The Wurst Case Scenario

Volume 11 of

The Casebooks

Of Octavius Bear

Harry DeMaio

"Alternative Universe Mysteries for Adult

Animal Lovers"

Paperback ISBN 978-1-78705-555-1
ePub ISBN 978-1-78705-556-8
PDF ISBN 978-1-78705-557-5

Published in the UK by MX Publishing
335 Princess Park Manor, Royal Drive,
London, N11 3GX
www.mxpublishing.com

Cover layout and construction by
Brian Belanger

Dedicated to GTP

A Most Extraordinary Bear

Acknowledgements

These books have evolved over a long period of time and under a wide range of influences and circumstances. I am indebted to many people for helping to bring Octavius and his cohorts to the printed page. Thanks most especially to my wife, Virginia, for her insights and clever suggestions as well as her unfailing enthusiasm for the project and patience with its author. To my sons, Mark and Andrew and their spouses, Cindy and Lorraine, for helping make these tomes more readable and audience friendly. To Cathy Hartnett, cheerleader-extraordinaire for her eagerness to see this alternate universe take form. To Jack Magan, Paul Bernish, Dan Andriacco, Amy Thomas, Luke Benjamin Kuhns, David Marcum, Derrick Belanger, and Zohreh Zand for their enthusiastic encouragement.

Kudos to Jim Effler, the late Bob Gibson and Brian Belanger for their wonderful illustrations and covers. Thanks, of course, to Sharon and Steve Emecz and Timi at MX Publishing for giving Octavius et al. a great home.

If, in spite of all this support, some errors or inconsistencies have crept through, the buck stops here. Needless to say, all of the characters, situations, and narratives are fictional. Some locations, devices, historical figures and events are real.

Also by Harry DeMaio

The Octavius Bear Series – Books 1 to 10

The Development of Civilization Volume Eleven - Part One

Our Origins

(From "An Introduction to Faunapology" by Octavius Bear Ph.D.)

About 100,000 years ago, according to scientific experts, a colossal solar flare blasted out from our Sun, creating gigantic magnetic storms here on Earth. These highly charged electrical tempests caused startling physical and psychological imbalances in the then population of our world. The complete nervous systems of some species were totally destroyed. For example, "Homo Sapiens" lost all mental and motor capabilities and rapidly became extinct. Less developed species exposed to the radiation were affected differently. Four-footed and finned mammals, birds and reptiles suddenly found themselves capable of complex thought, enhanced emotions, self-awareness, social consciousness and the ability to communicate, sometimes orally, sometimes telepathically, often both. Both speech production and speech perception slowly progressed with the evolution of tongues, lips, vocal cords and enhanced ear to brain connections. Many species developed opposable digits, fingers or claws, further accelerating civilized progress. Some others (most fish and underground dwellers) were shielded from radiation and remained only as sentient as they were before the blast. This event is referred to as The Big Shock. It remains under intensive study.

Positive in our knowledge that we are not alone in the cosmos, my staff and I are heavily engaged in Project Multiverse, successful searches for alternate universes, especially those in which "Homo Sapiens" continues to live and hopefully, prospers. This book also presents some of the results of that project.

The Players

- **Octavius Bear** – Mega-sized Kodiak; Narcoleptic war hero; Consulting Detective; Scientist; Inventor; Seeker of Justice; Gazillionaire owner of Universal Ursine Industries; Gourmet/Gourmand; Bee Keeper; Somewhat sedentary and grouchy just on general principles.

- **Mauritius (Maury) Meerkat** – Narrator; Assistant to Octavius; Theatrical Agent; African *émigré* with a French-Dutch background; clever with a shady history.

- **Bearoness Belinda Béarnaise Bruin Bear** *(nee Black)* – Gorgeous polar superstar, with the Aquashow, ***"Some Like It Cold;"*** Wife of Octavius; Extremely rich widow of Bearon Byron Bruin living in Polar Paradise in the Shetlands; Owner-pilot of the last flying Concorde SST.

- **Arabella Bear** – Hybrid bear cub prodigy; Twin daughter of Bearoness Belinda and Octavius.

- **McTavish Bear** – Hybrid bear cub prodigy; Twin son of Bearoness Belinda and Octavius.

- **Mlle Woof** – Bichon Frisé – Governess to the twin cubs.

- **Frau Schuylkill** – Octavius' beautiful Swiss she-wolf estate manager/cook/pilot/security officer with many other mysterious and military talents. She rescued Octavius from his dive off the Breakurbach Falls while he was struggling with his nemesis, Imperius Drake.

- **Wyatt Where** – Another wolf; Former military intelligence officer who had retired to a security post at the Bank of Lake Michigan in Chicago and then quit to join Octavius; Mate to Frau Schuylkill.

- **Howard Watt** – Porcupine; High tech security authority who also left the Bank to join Octavius; Alternate Universe specialist; Laser and particle beam accelerator expert.

- **Otto the Magnificent – aka Hairy Otter** – An absolutely terrible illusionist magician, Otto the Magnificent escaped the claws of super villain Imperius Drake but not before he developed some amazing powers courtesy of Imperius' genetic alterations.

- **Benedict and Galatea Tigris** – White Bengals; The Flying Tigers; Pilots of Belinda's and Octavius' aircraft; brother and sister.

- **Wolford Wolverine** – UUI and Octavius' personal Lawyer

- **Chief Inspector Bruce Wallaroo** – Irrepressible but brilliant marsupial; an international law and order genius from Down Under; often calls on Octavius and Maury for support.

- **Chita** – Beautiful, fascinating, clever, sexy, immoral and highly independent feline who among other things, is the publisher and editor-in-chief of *PURR* and *SOW* magazines.

- **L. Condor** – Andean Condor; cybernet genius with a twelve-foot wingspan and artificial voice.

- **Marlin** – Dolphin (sic) the Prince of Whales' Chief Scientist; Magician and part time Jester.

- **Doctor Llewellyn Llama** – Director of the UUI *Pharm and Pharma* Division.

- **Victoria Vicuna** – Llewellyn Llama's Personal Assistant.

- **Lewis Llama** – Llewellyn Llama's Brother.

- **Doctor Jacques Jackrabbit** – Assistant Director – UUI *Pharm and Pharma.*

- **Ormand Oryx** – Marketing Director – UUI *Pharm and Pharma.*

- **Serena Serval** – Lawyer – UUI *Pharm and Pharma.*

- **Rachel Raccoon** – Chief Biologist – UUI *Pharm and Pharma.*

- **Paul Possum** – Chief Process Engineer – UUI *Pharm and Pharma.*

- **Roland Reynard** – Executive Chef – UUI *Pharm and Pharma.*

- **Clarence** - Chinstrap Penguin - CFO *Pharm and Pharma.*

- **Roger Rottweiler** – CFO of UUI.

- **General Turmoil** – Horse – Leader of The Business – Intent on Cosmic Conquest.

- **Colonel Jupiter** – Horse – General Turmoil's Adjutant.

- **Lucinda Turmoil** – Horse – General Turmoil's Wife.

- **Clarissa Mare** – Horse – Lucinda Turmoil's Maid.

- **Lt. Sonia Sylvestris** – DC Metropolitan Police – Criminal Investigation Division.

- **Ursula 10** – Universal Ursine Intellect Model 10 – Artificial General Intelligence System.

Locations

Cincinnati, Ohio; UUI, Kentucky; College Park, Maryland;

Middleburg, Virginia;

Washington DC; and Alternate Universes

Octavius

Prologue

Do Bears give you a scare? Well, me too.
So, I'll pass on this tactic to you.
You just fix that old Bear
With a cold, piercing stare.
But make sure that he's Winnie-the-Pooh.

Hello again or first-time greetings to new readers of the Casebooks of Octavius Bear. I am Mauritius (Maury) Meerkat, sidekick to Octavius Bear and your genial host and narrator. Delighted to welcome you to Volume Eleven – *The Wurst Case Scenario*.

Octavius and I, accompanied by our two magnificent wolf associates, Frau Schuylkill and Colonel Wyatt Where, had just arrived back at the Bear's Lair, his opulent mansion near Cincinnati from a cinematic sojourn at Polar Paradise, the Castle/Resort owned by his wife, Bearoness Belinda Béarnaise Bruin Bear *(nee Black.)* Belinda, in order to retain her Bearonial status, must occupy the castle at least six months of the year. She and Octavius do high speed commutes between their spectacular homes in Cincinnati and the Shetlands, accompanied by their twin Cubs, Arabella and McTavish, and the Cubs' governess, Mlle Woof. You will meet the Fabulous Furballs, shortly.

As I said, my name is Maury Meerkat - also known as Offscreen Narrator. When I am part of the action, I am Octavius' trusted associate and field captain. I am two feet tall plus tail and I weigh in at twenty-four pounds. He, on the other hand, is a huge Kodiak – over nine feet tall and 1400 pounds – and like many of his species, is given to emotional outbursts.

You may also know that Octavius, among his many skills and accomplishments, is a brilliant, self-taught practitioner in the wide-ranging fields of biology, physics, ursinology, voodoo, teleology, chemistry, apiculture and oenology. He is a self-made gazillionaire and sole owner of UUI *(Universal Ursine Industries.)* He is also a first rate electrical, electronic, structural, marine, computer, communications, aeronautical, civil, mechanical and chemical engineer. He has a few other interesting characteristics such as falling into brief, deep narcoleptic comas – side effects of his successful genetic experiments to eliminate the need for him to hibernate.

However, the talent and occupation that should interest you most is his avocation for criminology. The Bear works in close concert with Inspector Bruce Wallaroo from Australia, of whom more later, and with his own Cincinnati based team – The Octavians:

- Frau Ilse Schuylkill – Swiss she-wolf; Bear's Lair estate manager; Cordon Bleu chef; jet pilot and sharpshooter with other very strange and arcane abilities.
- Colonel Wyatt Where – Another wolf; ex-military hero; security specialist and pilot; Frau Schuylkill's equally bizarre running mate.
- Doctor Howard Watt – Porcupine; brilliant scientist and technologist; laser and weapons specialist; Multiverse expert and Quantum Mechanics genius.
- Marlin – Dolphin from the Court of the Prince of Whales and Howard Watt's associate.
- Hairy Otter aka Otto the Magnificent – An absolutely terrible illusionist magician, Otto the Magnificent escaped the claws of super villain Imperius Drake but not before he developed some amazing powers courtesy of Imperius' genetic alterations. An alternate universe traveler.
- L. Condor – Andean Condor; cyber-net genius with a twelve-foot wingspan and artificial voice.
- Ursula – Universal Ursine Intellect Model 10 – Artificial General Intelligence System. (AGI)
- Your humble servant – African Meerkat; Octavius' indispensable assistant; operative; scribe; overall facilitator; talent agent as well as a pretty clever detective, if I do say so myself.

When we are not out scouring the world for evildoers, in cooperation with local, national and international constabularies, we are headquartered in a rambling old mansion near Cincinnati which encompasses not only the Great Bear's opulent digs, but his massive laboratories and shops; his missile silo disguised as an Asian pagoda; *(Don't ask!)* and a giant Roman temple that serves as a hangar for his four airplanes, a Twin Otter; a F15E Strike Eagle; a V-22 Osprey; a C5A-The Ursa Major; plus an AgustaWestland AW101 VVIP luxury helicopter - The Ursa Minor.

Across the Ohio River in Northern Kentucky, sit the headquarters, labs and some production facilities of UUI. Our story will take us there momentarily.

Howard Watt and Marlin have been back here at the Bear's Lair holding down the fort and pursuing their Multiverse Quantum Physics experiments. I shall bring you up to speed on their developments erelong.

The rest of our team including the Bearoness, Cubs and their governess. are just wrapping up shooting the interior scenes for a swashbuckling extravaganza in Moscow as part of a "film-within-a film" that had its origins at Polar Paradise. The guiding genius for this spectacular was none other than Preston Pavel Polar, superstar of a number of world-wide spectaculars starring himself and an assortment of Polar ingenues. Unfortunately, the 'ingenue du jour' for this film, one Brittany, exited her suite in the hotel by way of a bent balcony railing and landed in the ocean below – quite dead. Aided and abetted by international constabularies and consulting detective, Fetlock Holmes, we were able to find the culprit and see to the satisfaction of justice.

We had arrived at the Bear's Lair in Octavius' huge C-5A, The Ursa Major. We expect the Moscow members of the team to join us in a few days via the Bearoness' Aquabear, the last SST Concorde aloft. A happy reunion is planned under the culinary direction of Frau Schuylkill, a Cordon Bleu Chef. The Cubs will no doubt turn the event into a minor riot – their specialty.

Now let me take a moment and introduce a highly essential and near-miraculous member of the Octavians - Ursula 10 – Universal Ursine

Intellect Model 10 – Artificial General Intelligence System. (AGI) I'll let Ursula 10 explain herself.

"Thank you, Maury. Hello everyone!! My official nomenclature is Universal Ursine Intellect Model 10 – Artificial General Intelligence System. Ursula 10 for short. My predecessor systems were developed by the Advanced Super Computing Center at UUI. I am the result of the Computing Center team using those earlier versions to create a further enhanced entity-the Model 10. We are working together on a Model 11 which in turn will help produce even more sophisticated, independent and powerful AGI systems. Each advanced unit contains the capabilities, memories and power of its progenitors so in a sense, we are not replacing but rather expanding the Ursula family. While I am physically supported by a highly secure and hyper-powered server farm back in Kentucky, I also exist in clouds and network-based nodes and can be simultaneously incorporated into a wide variety of independent devices like this laptop unit here at the Bear's Lair. I combine quantum computing elements with very high velocity conventional circuits. My extremely high-speed multi-tasking abilities allow me to continuously serve a very large number of entities while simultaneously and independently enhancing my own abilities.

Depending on my physical platform, I can see, hear, feel and smell. I speak and understand an almost infinite number of languages and dialects. I can change my appearance and my vocal output to suit most moods and situations. I can interact with other devices, vehicles and structures and of course, all varieties of sentient animals in this world. I am also an important component of the Multiverse Project and am adapting my capabilities to deal with alternate universes as they are discovered. I have restraining functions which prevent me from doing deliberate harm even in self-defense, unless I am released by a recognized authority using very carefully protected clandestine codes. Finally, I have been told that although the Model 10 is shy on emotions, I have developed a finely-honed sense of humor. LOL!"

(Ursula has other capabilities such as breaking all known encryption codes and piercing deep personal identification techniques that we don't talk about publicly.)

Our team no longer believes she is magical or supernatural. I'm not sure what she is. Her personality gets more socially adept every day and she has taken to anticipating our interactions. Stay tuned.

Chapter One

While we're having a drink with the Bear
Fresh disasters descend on his Lair.
First an ally's passed on
Then his rival is gone.
Yes, the General's left but to where?

Octavius, Colonel Where and I were just settling down with an afternoon drink. The Frau was in her kitchen, planning out dinner with her culinary staff. She would, no doubt, join us shortly. The one non-drinker in the group, Ursula, was running in passive, silent mode when suddenly she rang her chime to get our attention.

"Yes, Ursie," I said, "What's up?"

"Some very bad news, gentlebeasts. UUI Human Resources and Security jointly report the death of Doctor Llewellyn Llama, Director of our *Pharm and Pharma* Division. His body was found in his hotel room in Washington DC by Victoria Vicuna, his Personal Assistant. The Washington Police believe he was poisoned. They are holding Ms. Vicuna for questioning."

Octavius snorted, "What was he doing in Washington?"

The AGI responded, "He was there to consult with the US Department of Agriculture and the Food and Drug Administration on our work on 'cultured meat' and artificial foods. It's not clear which government department has jurisdiction. Perhaps both."

"Another piece of news. General Turmoil is missing from his office in Washington. Interplanetary foul play or clandestine activity on the Business' part?"

The Great Bear looked at her and me. "One issue at a time! 'Cultured Meat' is one of our most controversial projects. Government, the Press, Science and Academia, all sorts of political and pressure groups, even churches, are taking sides and being damn vociferous about it. I told our PR people to keep me on top of any new developments. See if you can contact the DC Police."

Ursula interrupted. "That's not necessary, Doctor Bear. They are on the phone right now and want to speak with you. I am holding off the Press Corps, all of whom want a statement."

"Keep the Media at bay as long as you can. Get our corporate attorney, Wolford Wolverine in touch with Victoria Vicuna immediately. She obviously needs a defense lawyer who is a bright star in Washington and has successfully handled murder cases. They are calling it murder, aren't they?"

"It could have been an accident but that's something of a long shot. I doubt it's suicide."

"OK! Connect me with the Police."

The smartphone rang and a grizzled female mountain lion appeared on the screen. "Doctor Octavius Bear?"

"That's correct. I have two of my associates with me – Mr. Mauritius Meerkat and Colonel Wyatt Where (retired.)"

"Hello, Gentlebeasts! I am Lieutenant Sonia Sylvestris of The District of Columbia Metropolitan Police – Criminal Investigation Division. Do I understand correctly that you are the sole owner and CEO of Universal Ursine Industries?"

"That too, is correct."

"This morning, one of your executives, a Doctor Llewellyn Llama was found dead in his hotel room in downtown Washington. The preliminary conclusion by the Medical Examiner is that he died of botulism poisoning. The animal who found him is his Personal Assistant, Ms. Victoria Vicuna. She claims that he was late for a meeting at the Department of Agriculture and when she got no answer from his hotel room, she had the manager open the door with his pass-key. That's when they found his body and summoned us. We are currently treating Ms. Vicuna as a person of interest. No charges or accusations have been made as of yet. Ms. Vicuna had dinner with Doctor Llama last night and is the last animal known to have been with him before he retired."

"Lieutenant, we will have a lawyer on his way shortly to your offices to see Ms. Vicuna and to manage her release. She is hardly a flight risk and I will personally vouch for her availability. I plan to come to Washington first thing in the morning to help in your inquiry, if you'll have me."

"The Metropolitan Police are well aware of your reputation as a detective, Doctor Bear. As long as we can work out a mode of mutual cooperation, we have no objection to your joining in the investigation. I understand Doctor Llama was working on developing experimental foodstuffs."

"That's correct. That's why he was meeting with Agriculture and the FDA. I'll fill you in further when I arrive tomorrow. Meanwhile, I would greatly appreciate your working with our lawyer to help release Ms. Vicuna."

"I'll see what I can do. You can reach me at this number when you arrive."

They both hung up. "Well, Colonel. Looks like we'll have to haul out the Twin Otter for a trip to DC. Can you and the Frau be available tomorrow morning?"

"No problem, Octavius."

"And you, my little friend, want an airplane ride?"

"Sure!"

"OK, let's have dinner. Tomorrow is going to be a stinker."

Chapter Two

On a rather short hop to DC
The Great Bear was questioning me.
Would most carnivores eat
UUI's 'cultured meat'?
I don't know what the answer will be.

Very early next morning.

We are calling the Twin Otter into service for a brief trip to Washington. I guess we could have taken the Osprey or Ursa Minor, but Octavius has a place in his heart for the 'steady as she goes' Otter. The Wolves are in command in the cockpit and Octavius and I are seated in the main cabin, he in a chair specially designed to accommodate his 1400-pound girth and nine-foot height. I am ensconced next to him in a more conventional accommodation appropriate to my miniscule size.

Ursula 10, of course is with both of us. The Bear asked, "Ursula, bring Maury and I up to speed on recent events at the *Pharm and Pharma* Division. Why was Doctor Llama in DC at this particular time?"

The AGI responded, "It seems the division has staged several breakthroughs in the development of 'cultured meat.' They have been able to use cells taken from live animals and convert and propagate them into a base for edible meat products. They do no harm to the animals involved and form the foundation for growing an almost limitless number of cells for creating these products for carnivores. Doctor Llama was trying to set up procedures for obtaining government approval for the process and the products. There is a 'cultured' hamburger patty and a sausage. The Marketing Department wants to call them Best Burger and Best Wurst."

I chortled, "Someone has a weird sense of humor."

The Bear was not amused. "I remember that we were still fighting to assure product safety, fine flavor and getting costs down to a reasonable level. Have they succeeded?"

"Doctor Llama believed that once we entered mass production, we could get the price in line. Of course, regulation is a big issue. That's why he was starting government negotiation. The major question to answer is who has regulatory responsibility. It seems to depend on the proportion of meat in the products. The higher the content, the more it belongs to Agriculture. However, the first thing to determine is a definition of 'meat.' Lots of opinions on that one, too."

The Bear grunted, "I can see this one is not going to be easy and now with Llewellyn dead, things will be even more complicated. I know we are not alone in trying to create lab-based foods. Who are our nearest competitors?"

"Three large food companies – International Nourishment; Advanced Sustenance and Worldwide Brands; Taylor and West Central Agricultural Universities; SELB Labs; Farout Research; Biology Specialists LLC; The Carver Institute in the United States. There are dozens more overseas. The field is crowded but *Pharm and Pharma* is ahead of most of them in actual development."

"Maury, get on the horn to Jacques Jackrabbit, Doctor Llama's executive director and tell him I want a complete review of *Pharm and Pharma's* current status, plans and prospects when I return from DC. Special emphasis on the 'cultured meat' project. The media and the industry pundits will have a field day with this one."

"Ursula, check out the reactions of the scientific community and while you're at it see which political and religious entities have been negative on the project. Don't be surprised if there isn't a Congressional investigation launched. Thank goodness, UUI is a private company or we'd have stock analysts crawling all over us. As soon as we land, Ursula, bring the Wolves up to date on the situation. Also get all you can on botulism. How did it kill him? I want to know if any of the food samples he might have had with him could have contained the toxin."

Octavius then called our lawyer, Wolford Wolverine, who assured him that a local attorney had gotten Ms. Vicuna released on her own recognizance on the pledge by UUI that she would be made available to the Police as necessary. She would meet us at the morgue at eleven.

Octavius was clearly bothered by the whole situation. *Pharm and Pharma* is one of our top "growth potential" projects with possible world-wide impact. Llewellyn Llama was a personal friend of his. If his death was an accident, we had a lot of explaining to do. If it was suicide, which seemed highly unlikely, it would be even worse. If it was murder, we and the police both had an unsavory mystery on our hands. I didn't know which outcome to root for.

With that, Frau Schuylkill announced that we were approaching Washington National Airport and would be heading for the General Aviation Terminal. Given DC ground traffic, that meant we still had an hour or longer after we landed before we could get to the Mortuary at the Medical Examiner's offices.

The Development of Civilization Volume Eleven - Part Two

Feeding Carnivores in our Current World

(From "An Introduction to Faunapology" by Octavius Bear Ph.D.)

When the Big Shock took place 100,000 years ago, most of the world's mammals, avians, marsupials, reptiles and amphibians were affected. Because they were living totally beneath the water, which shielded them from the radiation, most fishes and invertebrates were not impacted. However, some sea dwelling mammals such as dolphins, whales and seals did go through the evolutionary changes outlined in Part One above.

As changes to personality, self-awareness, intelligence and physical versatility grew and we developed into our current states, replacing the now extinct homo sapiens, certain characteristics did not change. Paramount among these were digestive systems and thus eating habits. Herbivores remained plant eaters. Carnivores continued to seek meat for nourishment and the omnivores among us persisted in our flexible ways. Bears and meerkats are omnivores while wolves and dogs have strong carnivorous tendencies. All felines, including domestic cats, are obligate carnivores which means they should only eat meat. Other mammals that are classed as obligate carnivores include dolphins, seals, sea lions and walruses. Non-mammal obligate carnivores include salmon, hawks, eagles, crocodilians, many snakes and lizards and most amphibians.

Therein, of course, lies a serious problem. Carnivores were now seeking nutrition by eating <u>sentient</u> animals. This need set off a series of attacks, raids and wars that have lasted to this day. A number of individuals, societies, religions, countries and international organizations have made attempts to deal with the problem. Their solutions ranged from forced abstinence to killing off wounded, deformed or insane members of individual species for food. Many omnivores turned to an increased diet *of non-sentient animals such as fish who had not been enhanced by the effects of the Big Shock. This has resulted in a marked depletion in the aquatic population throughout the world. It has been theorized that the overall number of carnivorous animals has also been reduced due to lack of sufficient nourishment.*

Science to the rescue! In recent years, great strides have been made in laboratories and research test centers in developing what are known as "cultured meat, clean meat, artificial meat, lab-grown meat" and a host of other names. Unlike vegetable-based substitutes, these substances are developed and grown from animal cells taken from live and healthy species without harming them. Such are the research programs of UUI's Pharm and Pharma Division designed to sustain carnivores and some omnivores without engaging in cruel slaughter of sentient animals.

Chapter Three

The Bear stands there shaking his head
Llewellyn is certainly dead.
Now, how did he die?
And for that matter, Why?
Was he meant to be threatened instead?

The trip to the Office of the Medical Examiner's Morgue on E Street took a little less time than we had supposed, and we arrived at quarter to eleven.

Lieutenant Sonia Sylvestris along with a representative of the Medical Examiner's office took us down to the floor containing Doctor Llama's body. His brother Lewis Llama, just in from North Carolina, and Victoria Vicuna were already there. They had positively identified the corpse, but the Lieutenant asked Octavius to confirm the identification. Octavius shook his head, "Poor Llewellyn, a brilliant, highly energetic animal who devoted his life to nutrition research. It's ironic that he died of botulism."

He looked at the Medical Examiner's representative and asked. 'Doctor, what is your confidence level that it was indeed botulism that killed him?"

"Very high, Doctor Bear! We found significant amounts of botulinum toxin in the body and the post mortem indicated he had suffered from muscular and nervous failure."

"Was the toxin food-induced?"

"We haven't yet found any evidence of that. We are checking the guest lists of the hotel restaurant where he ate for other possible sufferers. He and Ms. Vicuna had the same dinner. Salad greens mixed with several types of grain. She is showing no symptoms."

I popped up. "Is botulism contagious?"

"From animal to animal, no! Of course, if food is the culprit and it is shared, it may seem contagious. In any event, it's a rather rare occurrence. We see it very occasionally as a result of injection."

"Any sign of an injection?"

Victoria answered, "Yes. Unfortunately he suffered from diabetes and needed shots twice a day."

The doctor shrugged. "One of those shots could have had botulinum toxin substituted for insulin. The effects would be slow but fatal."

"He didn't take insulin. It doesn't work with Type 2 diabetes. It was something else."

"Could the toxin have come from some of the lab samples he had with him."

Victoria responded, "He didn't have any samples with him. Part of the purpose of this trip was to get the regulators to send their scientists to *Pharm and Pharma* to start tests and inspections."

"So the toxin wasn't accidentally self-inflicted?"

"Not if you mean he tasted 'Best Burger' or 'Best Wurst.'"

The name induced some smiles in the group.

Octavius turned to the Llama's brother and asked, "Was Llewellyn married? We had no indication that he was."

"His mate died several years ago. She was a lovely Vicuna. He adored her."

Victoria sobbed and said, "She was my aunt."

Octavius looked surprised. "I didn't realize that you and Llewellyn were related."

"Only indirectly. He was kind enough to offer me a job when I left college. He was also supplementing my salary to help me get a master's degree. I'll miss him very much."

"Lewis, what do you do?"

"I'm an associate professor of mammalian biology at the University of North Carolina. I have a PhD and worked briefly with Llewellyn at UUI on a research project he was conducting into carnivorous digestive systems."

Lieutenant Sylvestris broke in at this point. "We will have to hold the body for a day pending a coroner's inquest, Doctor Llama. Can you arrange to stay here in Washington? The same for you, Doctor Bear and Ms. Vicuna."

Affirmative head shakes all around. I had already arranged hotel space for our team and Vicki Vicuna. I invited Doctor Llama to join us at UUI's expense. The Wolves had arranged to keep the Twin Otter at National Airport overnight.

The Lieutenant came over to me and the Wolves and introduced herself. Octavius had neglected to do the honors. She then asked us to accompany her back to Police Headquarters. In keeping with one of my normal assignments, I offered to buy lunch and asked her where we could go. The Morgue representative excused himself and set about returning the Llama's cadaver to its location.

The wildcat rubbed her whiskers. "This one seems very strange."

I chuckled, "You are a mistress of understatement, Lieutenant."

She smiled. "We 'obligate' carnivores are very interested in your project, Mr. Meerkat. It would make our lives considerably easier. You can't know how much pressure we get from do-gooder groups who would rather see us starve than eat meat. There have been several projects, including one of yours, to alter our digestive systems. I think that was the one Doctor Lewis Llama was referring to. All failures, so far. I have to keep my personal feelings to myself and remain the objective cop, but I was hoping the Best Burger-Best Wurst project would be a big success."

I replied, "It may yet be. We have a deep research team and plenty of money and resources behind it and Llewellyn wouldn't have been going to the regulators unless we had some pretty high confidence in its success.

Sorry to have this conversation right now, but let's go have lunch. The restaurant has a good seafood menu."

As we were walking out the door, Octavius pulled me back. "Since we have to stay here in Washington for the Coroner's Inquest, I'd like to use some of the time poking into the situation of General Turmoil. Is he still missing? Check with Ursula and then contact Colonel Jupiter, his second in command. Don't mention Ursula. We don't want them to know she exists. See if you can get the Colonel to meet with us."

(General Turmoil is a Horse. We call him Crazy Horse. He leads a clandestine, ostensibly non-existent, semi-governmental agency known as the Business. He and his group have a very high level of interest in the Multiverse and have the resources to go with it. Although he denies it, his apparent motivation seems to be conquering the cosmos.)

Ursula had told us: "General Turmoil is missing. No one has a clue."

"How do you know all this?"

"Oh, Maury, come on! Need you ask?"

"Sorry. Ms. Omniscience. So what's happening?"

"The General's second in command, Colonel Jupiter, who is also a horse, has been stirring up the security types. The search is on. Now, either they are engaging in some elaborate play-acting to cover up a calculated plot or someone has captured or done the General in.

Special Agent Maury on the trail of the missing horse. With a little help from my AGI friend, and after going through a lengthy spook rigamarole, I finally reached Colonel Jupiter.

"Yes, I know who you are, Mr. Meerkat. I wonder how you got to me."

"We, too, have our ways and resources, Colonel. I have been reliably informed that you are in search of the General who has gone missing."

"No comment!"

"Can you join Octavius Bear and me for dinner this evening. We are here in DC."

Long pause. Intake of breath. Soft whicker. "All right. I'll call you back with a place."

Bearoness Belinda
Béarnaise Bruin
(nee Black)

Chapter Four

Our schedule was filling up fast
The hours were just flying past.
More meetings were on
Where's the General gone?
Would we find out that answer, at last?

After we had all registered at the Fairfox Hotel, Victoria begged off dinner saying she wanted to meet an old classmate. Octavius warned her not to discuss the Llama situation although it had already reached the press. I suspected his warning would go unheeded. We would meet her again for breakfast and then proceed to the Coroner's Inquest. The following day, we planned to fly back to the Bear's Lair in Cincinnati, taking her with us.

Octavius, the Wolves and I had settled into the large sitting room of his suite, making a dent in the drinks table provided by management. Ursula rang her chime and two small multi-colored ursine faces appeared on her screen. The Cubs!

"Hi Poppa, Hi Uncle Maury, Hi Frau and Colonel! We're here in Ma's-cow. There aren't any cows but that's what they call this place. We don't know who Ma is, either. We've been in the movies. There are studios and big sound stages. Momma and Aunt Bearyl are film stars. Uncle Condo and Uncle Otto were both very funny. Preston Polar is very brave and wins all his swordfights. He thinks the films will be big hits. Just a minute, here's Momma." *(See Book Ten – The Camera Case)*

Belinda appeared on the screen after shooing off Arabella and McTavish. "Hello! It seems you've been busy since you returned to Cincinnati. I gather you're in Washington right now. Ursula gave us a briefing. I'm sorry to hear about Llewellyn. I met him once or twice and liked him. A fine gentlebeast. What are your plans?"

"We'll be returning to Cincinnati after the Coroner's Inquest here. We're not very far along in trying to untangle this affair. All we know for sure is he died of botulism but the how, why and by whom are all still mysteries. We do believe it was murder. Not enough evidence to support accident or suicide. How are all of you doing? The Cubs seem to be their usual energetic selves."

"Oh, how true! Poor Mlle Woof is having a real time trying to keep them under control although I will say they were very cute in their walk-ons as my two children. All told, I think the films will be a success. Our investment should pay off. We'll be getting on the Flying Aquabear tomorrow and heading to Cincinnati. You may be home by then."

We have another mystery of sorts here. It seems General Turmoil is missing."

"That's no great loss!"

"Agreed, but I want to know the circumstances. His disappearance could have an impact on us and our work. In any event, we are having dinner tonight with his deputy, Colonel Jupiter."

"Now, that's a first. Be careful he doesn't poison you."

"He may suspect us of doing the same thing to him. He's picking the restaurant."

"I'm serious, Octavius. Be careful!"

"Don't worry. Maury and the Wolves will be with me."

"All the same."

"OK! I will. We'll see you soon. Pet the Cubs and say hello to Otto, Condo and Mlle Woof. I gather Bearyl was a smash."

"Yes, she was. So was Chita. She's got the floozy thing down pat. The Feline Felons will be a big hit.'

"As will you be."

"Thank you, I think we ought to hang a picture of you with the plaid suit and cigar in the reception area of UUI. Our Founder."

"Not on your life! That was one of the dumbest things I ever agreed to."

"Oh, come on Tavi, lighten up. You were hilarious. Gotta go! I have to get the Cubs ready for our flight."

The Wolves and I had been taking this conversation in while lapping up bowls of ambrosia, in my case, fermented coconut milk VSOP. I tried unsuccessfully not to laugh but Octavius looked my way. Before he could say anything, he keeled over and started snoring. His narcolepsy had kicked in. Saved for the moment! He'll be back shortly, though.

The phone rang. Colonel Jupiter with the name and location of the restaurant. He wasn't happy that there'd be four of us coming. I told him we'd pick up the tab. It didn't help. I doubt if he'll come alone. Anyway, we were on for seven o'clock.

Actually, of course, there would be five of us. Ursula would be with us in passive observer mode on my laptop. We definitely did not want to reveal her existence to the folks from the Business. She rang her chime to get our attention. Octavius slowly returned from slumber-land and the rest of us were getting refills from the drinks table.

I've never heard an Artificial General Intelligence unit clear its throat before but clear it she did. The lynx image avatar that she's been using looked a bit pensive. "I suppose we ought to spend some time theorizing about Doctor Llama's death before we get too deeplyinvolved in the missing General. I know you don't like theories, Doctor Bear, but at the moment, that seems to be all we have. My probability algorithms strongly suggest that the crime, if such it is, took place back at UUI. If injected, the botulinum toxin could take as long as twenty-four hours to kick in. He and Ms. Vicuna left their lab, flew to DC and arrived at their hotel in time for a late supper and then headed off to their rooms. Sometime in the night, he succumbed. I believe we have to start looking for our suspects closer to home."

"Did he meet here in DC with anyone before going to bed? Perhaps for a drink? He could have been trying to grease the skids for the next day's meetings with some of the FDA or Agriculture staff."

The Frau replied, "If he did, it wasn't at the bar in his hotel. I spoke to the bartender. He doesn't remember any llamas or vicunas being in there all evening. Besides, with his diabetes he had to be very careful of his drinks consumption. Llewellyn wasn't a tee-totaller, but he seldom drank. Besides, I'm sure he wanted to be at this best during the meetings."

Octavius snorted. "All right, let's leave the Washington end to Lieutenant Sylvestris and the Metropolitan Police. We'll concentrate on *Pharm and Pharma*. Ursula, can you reach Assistant Director Jacques Jackrabbit? Maury spoke to him earlier about giving us a status report on the 'cultured meat' program. Let's see what he has to say, if he's still in his office."

A brief pause while the AGI made contact. A long eared lagomorph appeared on the screen, took off his glasses *(nearsighted)* and squinted at Octavius whose bulk made him easiest to spot. "Good afternoon, Doctor Bear. Hello, Maury! I'm not sure I know the Wolves who are with you."

Octavius replied, "Jacques, please say hello to Frau Ilse Schuylkill and Colonel Wyatt Where who are both on my staff. We're down here in Washington following up on the death of Doctor Llewellyn."

"Oh God! How tragic! He's such a loss both personally and professionally. It's a real blow to *Pharm and Pharma* and to me. He was a very good friend. Is his brother with you? It must have been a real shock to Victoria."

"Yes, his brother is here to claim the body as soon as the Police release it. He's taking it down to North Carolina. Victoria is beside herself. Right now, she's with a former classmate here in Washington, no doubt drowning her sorrows. She'll be flying back with us to Cincinnati. I assume you can find a new job for her."

"Well, I have my own Personal Assistant but I'll certainly find a suitable position for her. Do you want me to step in and take on Llewellyn's position for the time being?"

"Yes, but the arrangement will be temporary until I can sort things out."

"Of course! I understand fully."

"Jacques, I want a top to bottom review of *Pharm and Pharma* as soon as I return. Special emphasis on the 'cultured meat' project. That's been your baby, hasn't it?"

"Yes, it has. I have beeen briefing Llewellyn steadily. I helped him prepare his presentations for the Agriculture Department and the FDA.

"By the way, why weren't you with him here in Washington? I would have thought you'd be a key player in the talks."

"We have a whole series of laboratory trials on right now. We both felt it was more important that I stay behind and supervise them. Llewellyn was primarily making arrangements for future agency reviews. I guess we'll have to postpone tomorrow's government meetings."

"You're right. Since you know the contacts at those agencies and I don't, will you take care of that?"

"Certainly. Should I plan to make the government presentations at a later point?"

"Get a few open dates in few weeks' time. We'll plan our next steps during our review day after tomorrow. Thanks Jacques!"

He cut the connection. He turned to me. "Do we have a time and place for the Coroner's Inquest?"

"The Office of the Medical Examiner at ten o'clock."

"OK, we still have a little time before meeting Colonel Jupiter. I assume Jacques will make the arrangements for our review. I want all of you there plus Wolford. *Pharm and Pharma* has its own attorney but I want the Wolverine there as well. This project has all sorts of potential legal liabilities. I also assume Marketing will be represented. We'll have to go over their plans with a fine tooth comb. "Best Wurst!" I can't make up my mind whether I like that or not. I'm sure the FDA and Agriculture will have plenty to say about our testing, production and distribution processes and we haven't even begun to consider overseas activities. We've already had a few rounds of opposition to several of the genetically modified organisms that we produce for plant eaters. Lots of noise and heat. Not much knowledge or common sense. I'm not giving up on this 'cultured meat', though. Too many obligate carnivores and victimized mammals are involved. It may be a money loser for quite a while but, damn it, it's important. Let's have another round of drinks and then go have dinner with a horse."

*****

The wolves had secured a light truck for navigating around Washington. Octavius, as he was wont to do, stretched out in the bed causing a number of drivers and pedestrians to stop, stare and scratch their heads at the sight of a massive black bear being so casually transported. We pulled up in front of the Chez Lafayette Café and a canine parking valet immediately bore down upon us. He started his welcoming spiel but paused and gaped as the huge ursine in the rear of the truck struggled to exit the enclosure. Colonel Where turned the ignition fob over to the dog *(of unidentifiable breed or breeds)* and went to assist Octavius. The Frau and I walked into the lobby of the fussily fashionable bistro where we were met by a roan stallion and a pair of red foxes. Colonel Jupiter had a puzzled look on his noble face that was allayed as soon as Octavius shambled in the door on all fours and then rose to his full nine foot height. Wyatt took up the rear.

He neighed and said, "Doctor Bear, I presume."

Octavius grinned, showing his array of extraordinary teeth and replied, "You presume correctly, Colonel Jupiter. These are my associates, Frau Ilse Schuylkill, Colonel Wyatt Where, (ret.) and Mr. Mauritius Meerkat. I think you have been in contact with Maury."

"I have indeed. Let me introduce my two aides, Major Aaron Vulpes and Captain Benjamin Canidae." The two foxes, who were out of uniform, nodded. These were not the the members of The Business I had dealt with in Boston when we were pursuing the avian assassins from Biosphere X. *(See Book Seven – The Suit Case)*

The Horse continued, "I have set aside a private room for our session. I hope you enjoy French cooking. Pierre *(It's always Pierre.)* is a true culinary artiste."

I looked sideways at the Frau who is a medal winning, Cordon-Bleu chef among her many other talents. She returned my glance and sniffed. Oh boy!

When we had settled at the table, making the usual adjustments for the sizes of the participants and then ordering aperitifs, Major Vulpes, who had been staring at Wyatt, blurted out. "We've met before, haven't we Colonel?"

Wyatt stared back and said, "I don't think so, Major. I'm sure I would have remembered."

The Colonel was playing with the truth. When he was still in the Army, he and several other officers had been assigned to the Business to participate in a series of experiments in travel to alternate universes. He had undergone a number of medical, physical, psychological and stress procedures. Ultimately they declared the program a failure. When two of his companions mysteriously disappeared, probably to ensure project secrecy, Wyatt escaped, briefly joined a group of mercenaries, took up a job as security officer at the Bank of Lake Michigan and ultimately joined the Great Bear.

What the Business scientists didn't realize was the program was not a total failure. Wyatt could and still does travel to alternate universes and is a highly important member of Octavius' Project Multiverse. The Business, especially General Turmoil, is not aware of his abilities and nobody has any intention of enlightening them. The Colonel had met Major Vulpes briefly during his 'training' but the Major seemed vague in his remembrance. Let's keep it that way.

After ordering his meal, Octavius looked around the room and asked. "Is this a safe place for a confidential discussion?"

Colonel Jupiter nodded. "The wait staff and the maitre'd are our employees. So is the chef."

"Are we being recorded?"

The Horse hesitated.

"I assumed so."

Ursula was in passive mode on my smart phone but there was nothing apparent to signify her presence. So when it came to keeping records, we were even, although I'd put my money on Ursula every time.

The Bear looked over and asked, "What happened to the General?"

"We honestly don't know. He's been gone five days now. We have Military Intelligence, our own security people and several other agencies pursuing all leads. His quarters are untouched. His vehicle is garaged."

"Do you think the Biosphere X crowd may have gotten to him? He wiped out quite a few of them."

"As did you!"

"Touché!"

"We have seen no signs of violence or capture. They're not a very subtle bunch. Have you had any further contact with them?"

"Not since they tried to bomb my mansion and UUI."

"How did you deal with that?"

"Secret but highly effective defensive measures. *(See Book Seven - The Suit Case)* OK, Colonel, let's level with each other. We haven't the slightest idea where the General is or what has happened to him. If you're trying to find out what we know, that's it. I would like your assurance that his disappearance has nothing to do with any plans he has for us. You know there has been little love lost between the General and me and between The Business and UUI. If he has truly disappeared and you want our assistance, I'll consider it although you already have formidable resources at your disposal. If not, let's finish this exceptional meal *(A wink at Frau Schuylkill)* and go about our separate ways."

"What has brought you to Washington, Doctor Bear?"

"The mysterious demise of one of my major executives. We are working on the issue with the Metropolitan Police. I assume your organization had nothing to do with it."

"It's the first we've heard of it. I'm sorry to hear about it."

"So are we. We'll get to the bottom of it. Thanks for your time, gentlebeasts. We'll take care of the bill."

Throughout this conversation, Major Vulpes couldn't keep his eyes off Colonel Where but so far the penny hadn't dropped. We decided to leave before it did.

*****

Next morning, The Coroner's Inquest came and went as a formal non-event. No new information of value was revealed and the decision was death by misadventure, murder or culpable accident. The decision hung on the insertion of botulinum toxin in one or more of Llewellyn's diabetes injections. Victoria Vicuna related her discovery of the body along with the hotel manager. None of us believed it was an accident. Nor did we believe the injection was tampered with in DC. Lieutenant Sylvestris took up the local investigation. Llewellyn's body was turned over to his brother for burial in the family plot in North Carolina. We picked up the tab for transportation. Several representatives of the *Pharm and Pharma* staff including Jacques Jackrabbit would be attending the funeral. I volunteered to attend as well along with Victoria. We requested and received permission to take Llewellyn's paper work and materials back to UUI.

Mid-afternoon, we were ensconced in the comfortable seats of the Twin Otter and on our way back to the Bear's Lair near Cincinnati. Victoria seemed awed by her proximity to Octavius and his staff as well as the luxurious fittings of the airplane.

"Thank you, Doctor Bear for all you are doing. I suppose I no longer have a job at *Pharm and Pharma.*"

"On the contrary, Doctor Jackrabbit has committed to finding you a new job commensurate with your former assignment. Let me know how it turns out.

Chapter Five

The arrivals proceeded apace
With young travelers dropping from space.
The Cubs went sniffing for food
In a ravenous mood
And in general, upset the place.

When we arrived at the Bear's Lair, the Flying Tigers and ground crew were just pushing the Aquabear SST into the Roman Temple hangar under the wing of the giant Ursa Major C-5A. The Bearoness and her entourage had arrived. As we taxied up to the mansion, two fur covered meteors came dashing out the door, heading right for the Twin Otter. Frau Ilse tromped on the brakes and gunned the engines. The Cubs got the message. Back off!

Victoria, who had been awed all afternoon, looked out the window in amazement. First at the aircraft in the hangar, then at the mansion and then at the stream of animals coming out to greet us.

"Oh, Maury. I've never been here before. *Pharm and Pharma* and UUI are your typical scientific and industrial sites. This place is amazing."

"You ain't seen nothin yet."

The Bearoness walked over to the airstairs, accompanied by the prancing Cubs. Octavius struggled his way out of the expanded door of the Twin Otter, shambled down the steps backwards and on all fours, reached out and hugged his polar spouse and then the two mischief makers, accompanied by their governess, Mlle Woof.

Nobody was sure who was the welcoming committee since both parties had arrived almost simultaneously. Fortunately, Howard Watt, who with his associate Marlin, the Dolphin, had been keeping the Bear's Lair under control while everyone else was gallivanting around the globe, grabbed the ball and became the official host.

Frau Schuylkill, after turning the Twin Otter over to the Colonel and the ground crew hastened into the kitchens to begin a Cordon Bleu feast. The movie mavens assembled around Octavius and me. Otto, Condo, the Flying Tigers, Belinda, the Cubs and Mlle Woof. Bearnice, Leperello and Bearyl had stayed behind in Moscow to talk about appearing in another film. Chita and Jake the Jaguar had gotten off at Gatwick.

"Well, all you movie stars, are you ready to decompress or do you have a permanent case of 'film fever'? When are the Academy Awards?"

Arabella's ears perked up. "What are Alchemy Rewards. Poppa?"

Belinda laughed. "Academy Awards, dear. They're given out every year for Best Picture, Best Actor and Actress and other items."

"Well," said McTavish. "We'll certainly win them. Our picture is terrific."

"How do you know, mon petit? You haven't even seen it. It's not finished yet."

"It just has to be, Mlle Woof, that's all." the Cub replied. "Who is that?" he asked, pointing at Victoria.

Octavius snorted, "I'm sorry. Everyone, please say 'hello' to Ms. Victoria Vicuna. She was the Personal Assistant to Doctor Llewellyn Llama – Director of the UUI *Pharm and Pharma* Division. Doctor Llama unfortunately died on his trip to Washington to meet with the Department of Agriculture and Food and Drug Administration. Victoria discovered the body. His death is suspicious and is currently being investigated by the DC Police. I invited Victoria to fly back with us on the Twin Otter."

Belinda wrapped a paw around the vicuna. "Oh, I'm so sorry. I liked Llewellyn. That must have been a terrible shock for you. You'll join us for dinner, of course. Tavi, who is heading up *Pharm and Pharma* now?"

"Jacques Jackrabbit for the moment! I'm not sure he's the right choice for the job. He's a great scientist and renowned experimentalist but he's not as business oriented, politically astute or connected as Llewellyn was. He's the brains behind the 'Cultured Meat' program and we'd be in serious trouble without him, but I don't think he has much patience with bureaucrats. Please keep those comments to yourself, Victoria. Jacques is rather sensitive."

"Oh, certainly, Doctor Bear. If I learned anything in this job, it's to be discreet."

"Good!" Turning to the entourage, he asked, "How did the filming go? Do you think Preston Polar will have another blockbuster on his paws?"

Condo and Otto both nodded vigorously. The bird laughed, "It's tough to care for the guy but you have to respect his genius for show business. His films are as corny as can be, but they're done in a self-mocking way that sucks the audience in. He'll make money with this one and I guess you and the Bearoness, as his partners, are in for a big return as well."

Belinda smiled, "Which we'll distribute to all of you. We've asked Maury to alter your contracts to include profit sharing out of our portion of the worldwide revenues. Octavius and I don't really need any more money."

Grins, hugs and "Thank you's!" all around.

"OK," said the Great Bear, "let's see what culinary wonders Frau Schuylkill is coming up with. Victoria, you're invited to stay the night. One thing this mansion has is a lot of rooms. Tomorrow, we can get together with Jacques and see what can be done about getting you a new job."

"Oh, Doctor Bear, how wonderful!"

The evening proceeded smoothly and with as little ado as possible with the two Cubs in action. Otto was the first to ask. "What happened to Doctor Llewellyn?"

Octavius and I went through chapter and verse on the Llama's death and then switched over to our dinner with General Turmoil's minions.

Howard and Marlin both perked up on that one. The Porcupine squinched his nose and said, "I find it hard to believe that he voluntarily disappeared. Do you think the birds from Biosphere X are at it again?"

I replied, "It's a distinct possibility. If so, we may be next. Ursula, what do your probability algorithms have to say?"

The AGI, who had been operating in passive mode up to this point, paused briefly *(a first for her)* and then said, "I haven't picked up any hostile activity from them, have you Howard?"

"No! Marlin and I keep a watch on them, but I think they're too busy regrouping after the General's attack to launch any kind of a meaningful strike. That doesn't mean they couldn't have gone after the General, himself. Do you think Colonel Jupiter was telling the truth?"

"Tough to tell with those guys but they consented to our contact with them. That's unusual."

Ursula interrupted. "I think we're dealing with something altogether different. Did the Colonel say anything about there being any signs of violence in the General's office or quarters?"

"No, but I think their security folks would have covered that up if there had been any."

"Well," snorted Octavius, "that's their problem to solve. Just as long as we keep a watchful eye out for those screwballs on Biosphere X and ensure we're not in any danger, I'm content to let the Business handle its own business. Right now, I want to concentrate on *Pharm and Pharma.* Victoria, we're scheduled tomorrow to have a complete review of the division with Doctor Jackrabbit. When was the last time Llewellyn held a top to bottom assessment?"

"Oddly enough, Doctor Bear, it was only last week. I think he wanted to be sure of his facts before he went to Washington."

"Do you have the results of that review?"

"Only parts of it. There was a general conference with the managers and scientists and then Doctor Llewellyn and Doctor Jackrabbit had a confidential meeting. I only have the notes, charts and handouts from the first session. I'll get them for you. I don't know what happened in private."

The Development of Civilization Volume Eleven - Part Three

Synthetic Biology

(From "An Introduction to Faunapology" by Octavius Bear Ph.D.)

In these brief, compact essays that have appeared in all the previous books in this series, I have taken up a wide variety of subjects and issues to illustrate the progression of our civilization since the Big Shock. We've covered animal advancement, social norms, beliefs, politics, the arts, inventions and a far-reaching selection of scientific developments covering physics, chemistry, engineering, geology, astronomy, psychology and the like. However, I have had very little to say about biology, an omission I would now like to correct.

Any animal who has taken a high school biology class is familiar with the basics: Cells; proteins; amino acids; DNA and genetic codes, to name the dominant few. Until recently, study of biology has focused on defining, examining and tracking the natural progressions and relationships between these elements. While these examinations continue unabated, new, proactive efforts are being brought to bear that promise to immeasurably expand the biological universe and vastly impact animal-kind in the process. Enter "synthetic biology!" The UK Royal Society defines it as: "an emerging area of science that can broadly be described as the design and construction of novel artificial biological pathways, organisms or devices or the redesign of existing natural biological systems."

One-part research and one-part engineering, often merged! Proteins are at the center of all life. One estimate places nearly 5 million different proteins on earth. While they can be identified, there is no certainty as to what most of them do specifically. The cumulative effect is the nature of this planet. The interaction of amino acids with proteins yields an incredibly large set of alternative ingredients. One role of *synthetic biology is to meaningfully engineer the results of these combinations into new and useful substances. This has led so far to new forms of fabric; building and household materials; medicines and foods.*

Not all these efforts have been successful. Some results have been downright dangerous, but with appropriate safety and social provisions, the program is certainly worthwhile.

Our Pharm and Pharma Division has taken a leading role in these developments and will continue to dedicate major resources, talent and time to further explore and exploit the potential of synthetic biology. One such effort has been our work in creating 'cultured meat' with an eye toward meeting the digestive requirements of obligate carnivores without causing harm to innocent animals. Hence this story!

Chapter Six

Each thoughtful player will have a say
About which programs are underway,
On who would eat
Our 'cultured meat'
Octavian thinking was on display!

We relaxed in one of the Bear's Lair conference rooms – Octavius, the Wolves, Howard, Ursula and I – and waited for Victoria to bring in the materials from the recent *Pharm and Pharma* review. Otto and Condo were supposed to join us as was Belinda, if she and Mlle Woof could get the Cubs to settle down. Marlin was hooked up by closed circuit TV. I had taken charge of the drinks trolley and was doing my bartender duties when Ursula rang her chime and asked.

"Are we all agreed that Llewellyn's death was not a suicide?"

Howard and Marlin looked dubious but Colonel Where responded, "I think it's quite a stretch to assume the Llama might have deliberately overdosed botulinum. Why would he have the toxin in the first place? Where would he get it?"

Victoria had entered the room and picked up on the Wolf's comment. "To counteract neuropathy, Colonel. It's not completely out of the question that he'd have it. Botulism is one of the dangers inherent in food synthesis. We conduct intensive tests to ensure there are no accidents in the formulations. You would find toxin samples carefully preserved in the lab as a result of those tests. What I can't understand is how it would be packaged to be self-administered as an overdose by someone as knowledgeable and careful as the Director. "

Octavius snorted, "Highly unlikely. I think we can presume that someone tampered with his syringe or injected him with excess toxin when he was in a diabetic coma. Let's see what the DC Medical Examiner has to say. Meanwhile, Victoria, let's hear what the review sounds like."

The Vicuna brought up a Power Point presentation and said, "I was taking notes and I can't reproduce all of the discussion surrounding the slides. Each department head had 20 minutes to give a progress report and outline any new requirements, challenges and issues. As you can see, the major topics were building materials, medications, fabrics and foods. Since he was heading down to Washington on the following day, medications and foods occupied most of the Director's attention. Overall, the division's financial and marketplace prospects are quite favorable. A new line of industrial fabrics is about to be launched and is showing great promise."

Octavius turned to the AGI and asked, "Ursula, were you a party to the session?"

"Yes, Doctor Bear, and it came off as Victoria has described it with one exception. There seemed to be some discrepancies in several of the 'cultured meat' tests. Inconsistent tastes and textures. After the meeting, Doctors Llewellyn and Jackrabbit met in a private session. I wasn't a party to that. It must have been settled favorably because no alterations were made to the FDA and Agriculture notes or slides. Isn't that right, Victoria?"

"That's right, Ursula. I have those materials, too if you want to see them, Doctor Bear."

"I will, Victoria, but first, I want to hear from Jacques Jackrabbit tomorrow. I want all of you to sit in on that meeting and then I want to compare notes."

It was obvious the Great Bear had been quite perturbed by Llewellyn's death and was looking for any possible connections between it and the state of the *Pharm and Pharma* businesses. He seemed convinced that the botulism infection had originated at UUI. Several of us weren't quite sold on that theory…yet.

The Frau asked, "Did the Doctor have any personal enemies?" *(Basic Detection Question Number Seven - right after Who, What, Where, When, Why and How.)*

Victoria responded first. "If he did, he kept it to himself. I never heard him mention anyone and as far as I know, there were no threats or ongoing risks in his life."

Ursula spoke up. "Considering the nature and immense scope of what *Pharm and Pharma* is doing, there must be intense rivalries around every corner. There are some pretty ruthless animals out there. Anyone who was aware that Dr. Llama had appointments with government agencies would certainly conclude that we were making major progress in development. Those meetings are a matter of public record even if some information is confidential. We also have a stack of patents filed on the food and medicine programs. Killing off the Director could only be step one in slowing down our advances. I think we need to seriously enhance the security around *P&P* and that includes all of UUI and your group, Doctor Bear."

Octavius turned to the Wolves and said, "I agree. Sounds like you two have a new assignment. It wouldn't be the first time we've been under possible attack and this situation is far too volatile to treat lightly. I realize we already have a major protective program in place. You're doing a great job. But Llewellyn's death could be a warning signal. Get back to me in the next few days with suggested enhancements. The rest of you feel free to contribute as well."

Otto and Condo had joined the group and a somewhat flustered Belinda came in, blew out her cheeks and said, "I need a drink. I swear, Tavi, those two are getting more and more difficult to control. Poor Mlle Woof is at her wit's end. Now they want to set up movie studios here and at Polar Paradise. They have very serious cases of 'film fever.' None of this smartphone YouTube stuff for them. They want full-scale production facilities. McAra Studios. Arabella is writing scripts. *(Yes, she can write!)* and McTavish wants Uncle Maury to be their talent scout. They're looking to sign the Feline Felons, Bearnice, Bearyl and Lepi." She looked at Otto and Condo. "You two aren't safe either."

Uncle Maury gulped. From theatrical agent to bear cub talent scout. Ouch!

Octavius shook his head "They'll get over it. The Fad of the Week Club is at it again. Change of Subject: In spite of what I said, this disappearance of General Turmoil is bothering me."

Belinda said, "I should think you'd be relieved."

"I would be if I knew what happened to him and felt sure we weren't involved."

"Do you think Jupiter and his crew are telling the truth?"

"They're not saying much of anything. Straight stories are not their specialty."

"Then why did they agree to talk to you?"

"They're trying to figure out what we might have to do with it and what we know. I don't think we told them anything useful."

"Well, in the meantime, we have Llewellyn's death to wrestle with. You believe he was killed by someone here at UUI or *Pharm and Pharma*?"

"It seems the most likely scenario."

I interrupted. "What would be the most likely motive? If the culprit was looking to sabotage the 'cultured meat' project, there are more critical targets than the director. The program is still going on in spite of his death, isn't it?"

The Bear pawsed momentarily. "I certainly hope so. We'll see at tomorrow's briefing."

At this point, the door flew open and the two movie moguls made a swift and noisy entrance. "Poppa, did Momma tell you? We're going into the film business. McAra Studios. We're going to use all our friends and relations, aren't we, Uncle Maury? We have lots of room at Polar Paradise and here and we can rent all the equipment we need."

"Thank goodness you don't want to buy it."

"Is that Panda lady available? We're going to need a good photographer."

(They were referring to Jane Huang Hau who was involved in the filming of Preston Pavel Polar's swashbuckler at Polar Paradise. See Book Ten – The Camera Case.)

"We don't know, kids. Uncle Maury will have to find out."

Uncle Maury will have to pray that they lose interest and turn to something else like competitive beach volleyball.

Chapter Seven

For cultured burgers and lab-made wurst
A deep review is due, but first
The rest of things at P&P
Look very good for all to see
And healthy profits have been disbursed.

Over the river and through the trees, to UUI's house we go! We filed into the *P&P* conference room. Octavius, the Wolves, Howard, Otto, Condo, Victoria, Belinda, Wolford, the ubiquitous Ursula and me. We were accompanied by Roger Rottweiler, the CFO of UUI.

Jacques Jackrabbit and two of his research assistants were there plus *P&P's* lawyer, CFO and Marketing Director. The usual coffee and pastries were laid out on a credenza. Octavius wisecracked about whether the cakes were *P&P* products. They weren't. They were traditionally baked in UUI's kitchens. And they were good!

Jacques Jackrabbit stood next to a screen and kicked off the initial PowerPoint presentation. "As soon as this meeting ends, I will be going to North Carolina to attend Llewellyn's funeral. Maury, I understand you and Victoria will be coming too. I have arranged for the Flying Tigers to take us down, if that's all right with you, Doctor Bear."

The Great Bear nodded.

"Perfect! Let's proceed. First, Octavius, here is a view from 30,000 feet of *P&P 's* current status and a short-term business forecast. The first graph outlines our existing product set and the services associated with them. As you can see, several of our synthetic biology lines are quite profitable: fabrics; building materials and household supplies. We also produce several over-the-counter medicines. However, those synthetic products have been easier to bring to market because regulation in those areas is not as onerous as the medical space. We have found that while we have competition, we have been able to build market share steadily. Isn't that right, Ormand?"

Ormand Oryx is the Director of Marketing for *P&P*. The antelope shook his head affirmatively, rattling his long and slender horns. His black, brown and white face broke into a wide grin and in an unexpectedly deep voice, he said. "Our client list is getting bigger every day. We don't just sell our products. We service them. That keeps us in a tighter relationship. We've had several successful client conferences; trade shows and exhibitions and we're launching a new ad campaign for our fabrics and household supplies.

We have a major marketing program in the final planning stages for 'Best Wurst' and 'Best Burger.' Isn't that right, Clarence?"

The CFO, a Chinstrap Penguin named Clarence nodded his head in agreement. "Of course, a lot of that profit from fabrics, building materials and household supplies is going to fund the development side of our 'cultured meat' project.

The Great Bear looked at the Marketing Director and asked, "Who came up with that 'Best Wurst' title?"

"Our advertising agency, Little & Small. They've been with *P&P* for several years. Do you like the name? It's been heavily test marketed. We've conducted focus groups. The humor seems to take the edge off the synthetic meat concept. We've been trying to get rid of the word 'artificial.' We're using real meat cells grown first in labs, then in our production centers. The taste and 'mouth feel' are authentic. The obligate carnivores need to be convinced of that and assured that no harm was done to any animals in the process. Of course, that was a main part of the message Doctor Llama was going to deliver to Agriculture and the FDA."

The lawyer, Serena Serval, herself a unique cat and obligate carnivore, flicked her oversize ears. "That issue is political dynamite. Expect to be questioned by Congress and state governments; medical associations; religious, education and social organizations; do-gooders and the media. Pardon the humor but this is catnip for the press. We are arming ourselves with the best testimony we can obtain both here and overseas. This one will not be resolved easily."

Jacques Jackrabbit jumped in. "BUT, safety is our number one message. It's imperative that Llewellyn's death is in no way tied back to our products or processes. There is no way he could have succumbed to botulism through the 'cultured meat.' He didn't have any with him."

Octavius looked over at Victoria. "You can confirm that?"

"Yes, Doctor Bear. I helped him pack. There were no samples of any kind."

"OK! Let's get back to the subject at hand. I'm pleased with your progress with the non-edibles. But 'cultured meat' will be the make or break item in the *P&P* business model. Where do we stand on its development?"

The two research assistants, a biologist and process engineer, were waved up to the front of the room by the acting director. "Everyone, I want you to meet Dr. Paul Possum and Dr. Rachel Raccoon, the brains behind the Best Burger and Best Wurst projects. Rachel is a biologist par excellence. She and her team have done the science that defined and isolated the genetic enhancements and modifications required to produce synthetic animal cells. It's still a work in progress but enough advances have been made and recorded for us to turn the work over to Paul and his excellent engineers to build the development processes. We are sufficiently confident of our results to invite the FDA and Department of Agriculture to examine our work on a non-disclosure basis. Serena will manage the agreement process."

The Raccoon spoke up. "You are, no doubt, aware, ladies and gentlebeasts, of the immense number of amino acid-protein combinations in nature. Most of them have yet to be explored and very few of them have been reproduced in the laboratory. After a long progression of failed experiments, *P&P* has been able to replicate existing fabrics and materials and create previously non-existent substances. Some have already gone to market."

"Fortunately, our group has the specific mission to synthesize the cell structure of animal tissue. That narrows the options dramatically. For the moment we have chosen the cow and pig as our sources although we propose to expand our inventory as we progress. For example, we have made some as yet incomplete experiments with deer, chickens, turkeys and ducks. I must stress that at no time have we caused more than very minor discomfort to our subjects."

Paul Possum added, "There is also a project in the works to mass produce synthetic grains, tubers, roots, berries and leafy vegetables tailored to the needs and preferences of the herbivore and omnivore communities worldwide. These will be fabricated independent of climate, soil, water and natural chemicals in places heretofore regarded as unable to sustain crops. The potential is gigantic. Needless to say, there will be intense disagreement and possible conflicts."

Jacques turned to Frau Schuylkill and asked the she-wolf. "I understand, Frau, that you are a Cordon Bleu chef. I wonder if you could spare us some of your time and expertise and advise us in preparing some dishes made from Best Burger and Best Wurst? Much of our success depends on the taste and consistency of the products. Packaging and preparation are key."

Before she could give an answer which I believed would have been in the negative, Octavius intervened. "Of course, she can. Although she is a mainstay of our team, I believe she can be spared for some periods to share her culinary know-how. Ilse, you can pass on some of your aviation duties to the Colonel and the Flying Tigers. Belinda can probably be of help, as well."

The Frau was astute enough to understand that the Bear had a hidden agenda he wanted carried out. She somewhat reluctantly agreed but not before giving Octavius a searching stare. He simply nodded. She smiled.

Neither Rachel Raccoon nor Paul Possum seemed all that happy at the prospect but they wisely said nothing. This could get interesting.

The UUI CFO snuffled. Octavius looked at him and asked, "Yes. Roger, did you want to say something?"

The Rottweiler looked over at the Penguin and said, "Clarence and I have been holding joint meetings over the past several months to ensure *P&P's* financial reporting is consistent with accepted accounting procedures. UUI is investing a lot of venture capital in this division's programs and financial accuracy and completeness are critical. I don't have to tell you that we are at risk in spite of the success of the fabric, materials and household supplies endeavors."

"We don't anticipate profitable returns on the food projects for several years, if then. I am not suggesting we turn the programs off. Quite the contrary. I am a believer but I am a clear-eyed, cold-blooded believer. We didn't have a chance to fully discuss it with Llewellyn before his unfortunate death but I want to initiate an outside audit of the 'cultured meat' and other food projects. We are about to substantially accelerate our investment and expose ourselves to government scrutiny. We need to step cautiously. I think Clarence and Serena agree with me."

The Penguin and the lawyer both nodded. Jacques, Ormand, Rachel and Paul all looked shocked. Octavius and his team sat in silence as this discussion was going on.

The Marketing Director spoke up. "Why are we just hearing about this now? Were you going to let Llewellyn go to the government agencies while we were conducting an independent audit of the programs? If we go ahead with this, it will delay the project by months. I must protest. Jacques, Paul, Rachel. What do you think?"

Rachel spoke first. "Frankly, I resent this as an unnecessary intrusion in our development process. It is a typical bean-counters' reaction to something fantastically innovative that is expanding the horizons of world nutrition. We have been scrupulous in our research efforts, Doctor Bear. We felt strongly that Llewellyn was correct in taking the next step and opening the closet to the regulators. This audit will set us back immensely."

Paul Possum shook his head in agreement. "Pardon the pun but our competitors will be eating our lunch. We have made tremendous investments in staff, equipment, materials, software and facilities to launch these programs. And now we are going to blow our competitive edge. I'm appalled."

The Great Bear sucked in his breath, the equivalent of an F3 tornado, and said. "Well, we clearly have a major issue on our paws. Here's what I want to do. We will use Llewellyn's death as an excuse to regroup. I don't want that to take more than a week. Roger, I want you and Clarence to come back to me in three days with a definitive proposal for this audit. Jacques, you, Rachel and Paul will give me a detailed technical progress report on both Best Burgers' and Best Wurst's readiness for release. Frau Schuylkill will assist you. Ormand, I want a detailed and objective analysis of what impact postponements will have on going to market. We will all meet again in three days after Jacques, Maury and Victoria get back from Llewellyn's funeral. Meanwhile we have a mystery on our hands. Who injected Llewellyn with botulinum toxin and why? Do any of you have any comments or suggestions you wish to make on that subject?"

Paul asked, "He died in Washington. Doesn't that put Victoria here on the top of the suspects list?"

"No, it doesn't. The timing suggests he was poisoned here and the toxin took effect in DC The Police are of the opinion that someone tampered with his diabetes shots. We're not ruling out the possibility that it happened in Washington but it seems far more likely that UUI is where the switch took place. Thank you all for coming. This was much more interesting than I expected. I will see you again in three days. I'd like my team to meet with me back at the mansion in an hour." He rose and led the parade out of the conference room.

Chapter Eight

Suspicions are sure rising quickly.
Llewellyn was certainly sickly.
Then there's Ursula's hack.
Crazy Horse has come back.
And the rumors are flying quite thickly.

Octavius and I are on our way back to the Bear's Lair in the bed of his specially designed pick-up truck. The Wolves are in the drivers' compartment. The rest of our party is in an oversized SUV. He addressed Ursula. "Well, Ms. Omniscient, what's your take on all of this?"

"You need to do some deep digging, Dr. Bear. I don't think things are what they seem."

"You mean **_we_** need to do some deep digging."

"Of course! I wouldn't miss this for the galaxy."

I piped up. "I'm not sure I see the problem. I can understand Rachel, Paul and Ormand getting upset at the prospect of uninvited delays in the release process. In fact, I'm a bit surprised that Jacques isn't more troubled by the idea of an audit."

The AGI chuckled. "It may be just what he wanted. He may not believe that Best Burgers and Best Wurst are ready for prime time."

"Puns are not your strong suit, Ursula!"

Octavius picked up on her comment. "Do you think he might have killed Llewellyn to stall the project?"

"It's a possibility, Doctor Bear. Not very high on my probability estimates but still a possibility."

I asked, "Why do you think Roger and Clarence held off on until now to request the audit."

"They wanted to do it in front of me," said the Bear. "If I bought into it, there's be less overt resistance by the others. That won't stop some rearguard action, however.

"Where's the lawyer in all this?"

"Doing what lawyers do best. Playing it safe. I'm eager to see what Frau Schuylkill comes up with."

"Octavius, I think you need a few words with her. She is so finicky about food that she may overdo her resistance to the project."

"I'd agree but she is very sympathetic to the plight of the obligate carnivores. Plus, there is practically nothing she can't vastly improve with her culinary talents. But, you're right. I'll have a chat with her. I know she doesn't care for the assignment."

With that, we drew up to the Bear's Lair. The Cubs were waiting impatiently. "Poppa, Poppa, we found a place that rents film studio equipment and there's a big storage room in the basement of the mansion that we're going to use for a sound stage. Uncle Maury, we need a scriptwriter. We're going to make a movie about two brave and clever young bear cubs *(That's us!)* who fight off a gang of feline criminals who are holding a beautiful polar bear sow for ransom. *(That's Momma!)* Poppa, you play the rich gazillionaire who is her husband. The Colonel and Frau are your bodyguards. Uncle Otto, Uncle Condo and Howard are the Police. Can we get Uncle Bruce to come up from Australia? We haven't figured out a part yet for Marlin but we will. Aunt Chita, Lepi, Jake and the Flying Tigers are the bad guys! Isn't this great?"

They ran out of breath as did we. Mlle Woof was unsuccessfully trying to herd them back into the house.

The Great Bear looked up to the sky. "At least they don't want to use the airplanes."

"Don't count on it. You may have to buy or rent a couple of drones, if you're going to let them go ahead with this."

"I'm counting on you to talk them out of it, Maury."

Oh swell, all this while we find out who killed Llewellyn; what happened to General Turmoil; setting up internal meetings at *Pharm and Pharma;* digging into the Best Burger and Best Wurst programs and coordinating with the Washington Police. Just another dull, ordinary day in the life of a meerkat.

*****

At the appointed hour, the team gathered in the large mansion library to 'cross-pollinate' *(whatever!)* and polish off a few drinks. Victoria was still with us and Ursula was in active mode.

Belinda asked, "Victoria, did Llewellyn have any inkling about this audit proposal?"

"I don't think so, Bearoness, but I can't be sure. He certainly never discussed it with me and I didn't see anything about it in his recent correspondence. I don't remember him having any exchanges about it with Roger or Clarence."

"Do you have access to his e-mail, twitters and texts?"

"Only the business-related items. He kept personal materials on a separate, encrypted server. I never thought anything of it. After all, we're all entitled to our privacy, such as it is."

"Is there any way we can gain access to that server?"

"Not that I know of."

She wasn't counting on the power of Ursula 10. I'm sure the thought of Ursula's hacking abilities occurred to Octavius and several other team members. No one, including the AGI, said anything. Victoria had only the vaguest notion about Ursula. We wanted to keep it that way.

Ursula sounded her chime.

I responded. "You rang, oh Sagacious One?"

"Thank you! It's nice to be appreciated. Ms. Vicuna, what I am going to say should be strictly confidential."

Octavius intervened. "Victoria, I'll give you a choice. You signed a non-disclosure agreement when you joined *P&P*. That applies to UUI as well. I'm going to extend that to our current investigative activities. You can agree to keeping our discussions, discoveries and inquiries secret or you can leave now. No prejudice. No problems with your future employment. I believe you can be useful to our efforts but if you feel uncomfortable or worse, I don't want you on this team. You may have to comment on your fellow workers. If that's a loyalty problem, let's dispose of it now."

"Oh, no, Doctor Bear. You have been exceptionally kind to me and I want to repay you, if I can. I'll be happy to sign an agreement and you certainly have enough witnesses." She smiled at us.

"Good! Go ahead, Ursula!"

"I have searched the Director's personal e-mail server. *(Victoria looked shocked.)* In notes to Jacques Jackrabbit there are several mentions of an upcoming audit by Roger and Clarence. Llewellyn approved but wanted it kept confidential until it was actually announced in front of you and your staff, Doctor Bear. He suspects that some of the research data has been modified. He does not mention who he thinks is responsible. He decided to go ahead with the government meetings anyway."

"Did Jacques respond?"

"Just a 'let's discuss'."

"I think I have to have a one-on-one with Doctor Jackrabbit. Does anyone want to comment?"

"The Colonel snarled. "That would explain Rachel Raccoon's resistance to the audit."

"We can't be sure she is guilty of any wrongdoing" said the Bear. "We're not even sure there is anything faulty with the data. It's a suspicion. Just a surmise."

"If the results are flawed and Llewellyn could prove it, that might explain his murder."

"That thought occurred to me too, Maury, but let's not get ahead of ourselves. I want to get back to that botulinum toxin. Where could it have come from and who would have access to it?"

Victoria spoke up. "I'm afraid, Doctor Bear, that botulinum is one of the research substances used in the *Pharma* labs. They keep a controlled inventory of bacteria, viruses and parasites for comparative testing of potential sources of food poisoning in the experiments and process results. The government health and food control agencies will insist on carefully examining all samples submitted to them against a long list of possible toxic substances. I have had to prepare some of those lists and results for Rachel and Paul to turn over to Jacques and Doctor Llama. As to who might have access, I'm sorry but I don't think the controls on access were all that carefully imposed. The scientists and technicians had to sign out for them but I don't remember anyone ever being challenged. Of course, that isn't part of my responsibilities. Rachel Raccoon and Paul Possum keep the records."

"Well, let's add that to the list of questions we want to ask those two. Of course, the clostridium botulinum toxin may not have come from the *Pharm and Pharma* inventory. I'm sure there are other source labs where the toxin can be obtained. Run a check on that, will you Ursula."

"Of course, Doctor Bear!" *(A brief pause.)* "There are three medical labs that supply *Pharm and Pharma* with a variety of test capabilities, including finding poisonous substances. I shall have to check their usage logs for recent entries. That may take a few minutes. While I'm doing that, here's a piece of news. General Turmoil has been found."

The Bear snorted. "Dead or alive?"

"Oh, he's alive…after a fashion!"

"What does that mean?"

"I'm not quite sure. The whole affair is quite mysterious. The Business is being very secretive. I only found out about his reappearance from hacking their systems. He says he has no memory of what has happened to him over the past two weeks. Or he may be lying or blocking it. He just showed up again in his office this morning. No explanations."

"I wonder if he was on an alternate universe excursion." This from Howard.

The AGI retorted. "My probability algorithms tend toward that reasoning, Howard, but I don't think the birds of Biosphere X were involved. They probably would have killed him. This is something else."

I chortled. "That's the General. He's always been something else."

"Well," said the Bear, "let's keep a sharp eye on that situation but Llewellyn's death and the issues at *Pharm and Pharma* are our top priorities. Ursula and Frau Ilse, let's see what you can dig up on the Wurst projects. Something doesn't smell right and I don't mean the food."

Chapter Nine

The assessment is moving ahead
Though the techies all wish it was dead.
And the Cubs want to spend
Poppa's money no end.
Could Octavius go in the red?

On our way back from Llewellyn's funeral in North Carolina. Victoria, Jacques and I were sitting in the Twin Otter's opulent seats. The Flying Tigers - Benedict and Galatea Tigris - were in the cockpit guiding us over West Virginia on our way back to Cincinnati. The conversation was at an ebb.

I took it upon myself to break the ice. "I assume Paul, Ormand and Rachel are hard at work trying to make the assessment unnecessary. It must be frustrating for them to have their plans and processes cut off at the pass."

Jacques looked up at the ceiling and flapped his ears. "They'll survive. I want to be absolutely certain we haven't missed anything crucial in bringing the program this far."

"So you agree with Roger and Clarence that an audit is called for. Who will conduct it?"

"There are several labs we have been working with on a highly confidential basis and of course, Octavius will have to sign off on any of the participants."

"Did Llewellyn know about Roger and Clarence's concerns?"

"Not that I know of. We didn't discuss it."

Well, Jacques could lie with a straight face. I wasn't about to blow Ursula's cover. Maybe, Jacques just didn't trust me and decided to play his cards close to his furry chest. Something to discuss with the Great Bear.

Jacques changed the subject. Turning to Victoria, he said. "I've been thinking about your next position. You've had some very valuable experience in the Executive Office and I don't want it to go to waste. It isn't clear who will take Llewellyn's place permanently. It may or may not be me. I'm probably going to hold down two jobs for the time being. As Assistant Director, I've been handling the technical and development processes – a sort of Chief Operating Officer or Chief Scientist. My PA, Eleanor, is an excellent technologist and I want to keep her in that job. Llewellyn was the CEO handling the business aspects of *Pharm and Pharma*. If I have to handle that job as well, I'd like you to stay on in your current position. I hope the two of you will be able to work together."

Victoria replied, "I'm sure we can, Doctor Jackrabbit. She is a wonderful Eland and we've cooperated on projects before. Thank you for keeping me on, at least temporarily."

"If this audit comes off, the two of you will have to help administer the process. I'm sure Paul, Ormand and Rachel are going to be difficult to deal with."

I stuck my nose in. "I'll bet Octavius will have a few words to say on that subject. He can be very persuasive. Of course, he's very much taken up with Llewellyn's death."

Victoria sniffled – not the first time this day. The funeral had been a tearful affair.

A feline growl echoed over the plane's sound system announcing our approach to the Bear's Lair.

*****

As we taxied up to the apron, two brown and white streaks came bounding up with a curly haired white canine in pursuit. The Cubs seemed to have no fear of airplanes, moving or otherwise. A tug moved toward the Otter's nose wheel as the props wound down. The Fur Balls jumped up and down waiting for Galatea to lower the air stairs. I was no doubt their target with fresh news and requirements for McAra Studios. *(I wonder how McTavish got top billing.)*

"Uncle Maury, Uncle Maury! Chief Inspector Wallaroo is coming up from Australia and Aunt Chita and Jake are flying over from London. Isn't that great? We'll have the good guys and the bad guys for our movie. The Bold Brave Bears. Isn't that a terrific title? That's us, of course. Momma and Poppa play Momma and Poppa. We're keeping it simple! They are bearnapped by the bad guys and taken to another world. That's going to be shot at Polar Paradise. Howard and Marlin help us rescue them and bring them back. You get a part too, along with Otto and Uncle Condo. Can you talk the Frau and the Colonel into acting with us? We need the Panda Lady to take the pictures. You're not too busy, are you? Say you'll help us. Puh-leeze"

The real facts are that Octavius called on Bruce Wallaroo and Chita to do some sleuthing both on Llewellyn's death and the brief, mysterious disappearance of General Turmoil. If the Cubs could get some help out of them, so be it. Although I sincerely hoped this would be another short-lived enthusiasm on their part. If anything, the two of them know how to spend their parent's money.

"OK! Keep your fur on! I'll see what I can do. How did you rent all that equipment?"

"We used Poppa's credit card! That's what we always do. Sometimes we use Momma's."

Octavius will be delighted. I cornered the Great Bear *(or perhaps he cornered me.)*

"We have things to discuss." We said simultaneously. As usual he spoke first.

"I've asked Bruce to come up here and look into the General's disappearance."

"I know. You asked Chita to come over, too."

"How do you know?"

"Certain little ursine thespians have made me aware of it in addition to giving me a laundry list of requirements for "The Bold Brave

67

Bears." They've also been making fast and loose with your credit card in outfitting McAra Studios. Are you and Belinda going to play along?"

"Oh, what the Hell! It's only money!"

"Is now the time to hit you up for a raise?"

"No!" *(followed by a large snort)*

"I had a brief discussion with Jacques on the way back from the funeral. He denies having any discussions with Llewellyn about an audit. Ursula's hacking of his e-mail says otherwise. He's also going to keep Victoria on as the CEO's PA. Since he's going to hold down two jobs until you decide which way to go, he's going to keep an assistant apiece for each of his assignments. He wants them to help manage the audit if there is one. Will there be one?"

"Unless the marketing, research and development types can convince me otherwise, there will be. Of course, I want to hear what Clarence and Roger have to say. They're mostly concerned about the finances. I'm concerned about the viability of the "cultured meat" program. Call it ursine intuition but I'm not comfortable with the Best Burger and Best Wurst processes. We need an objective analysis. I want to hear what the protagonists have to say and then I want to interview these confidential labs to see if they can handle the audit. If they've been too deep in our development activities, I'm going to look elsewhere. Tomorrow's meeting will be very interesting. Have you set it up?"

"No, I've been busy at a funeral and pumping our Scientific Director." *(to say nothing of listening to the demands of our youthful movie producers.)*

"Well, get to it, Mr. Coordinator! Then we'll see about a raise."

"What's the story with Chita? Don't tell me you've given her a clean bill of health."

"No, but Chita has one essential plus for our investigations. She's a cat – a obligate carnivore. In analyzing the end products, I want Frau Schuylkill to apply her culinary skills and I want Chita to act as the experimental animal. I've spoken to her about it. Plus, she's got a real talent for sniffing out bad guys. Somebody here killed Llewellyn. I want to know who."

"Where does Bruce fit in?"

"He's going to play the Australian government card and set up a joint investigative project of extra-terrestrial activity with The Business. Let's see what comes of it. If anything!"

Chapter Ten

Advance Oh Australia Fair!
Here comes Bruce with his Down-Under Flair
With an Ursula pal,
A most erudite gal,
He'll have news for Octavius Bear.

I spent the rest of the day making sure tomorrow's *Pharm and Pharma* staff meeting to discuss the audit was in readiness. I got some pushback from Rachel who obviously resented the whole idea but the mention of Octavius' concerns and expectations got her back in line. Don't mess with a nine-foot Kodiak who holds your paycheck! Ormand and Paul claimed they were ready. So were Clarence and Roger. I got Ursula primed to operate in passive mode. Our team was to be Belinda, the Frau and Colonel, Wolford Wolverine, Octavius and me. Howard, Otto, Condo and Marlin weren't going to be there for this round. Jacques, the lawyers and the two PAs would of course be front and center. The primary topic was the Best Burger and Wurst products but the overall health of the organization was still up for discussion.

We also needed to vet the outside labs who would be conducting the reviews, if any.

Octavius also intended to slip Llewellyn's death into the conversation. Unfortunately, Chita had not yet arrived but she would be mentioned primarily in her role of obligate carnivore. Her inquiries into the Llama's demise would be presented as feline curiosity.

OK, time to report to the Great Bear. I may or may not bring up the subject of a raise for good old Maury. I'm sure the Cubs won't mind.

*****

Ursula's chime broke my concentration. "You rang?"

"Yes, Maury. I am in contact with Chief Inspector Wallaroo. He's in Washington. I have downloaded a copy of my persona onto his laptop and we are now in full communication. I will be happy to patch you through. Hold one moment, Inspector. I also have Howard and Marlin in the loop."

"Rightcheare, Ursie. G'Day Maury! Howard and Marlin, how you goin'? Greetings from the D of C. I'm bringin' an Aussie Government shout to the General and his partners in the Business. Canberra is very much interested in extra-terrestrial life. They know I've been involved in some of those capers and they want me to represent Oz to your government. Among the five of us, I'm trying to find out what the General is up to. I understand he did a bunk for a couple of weeks. Any idea where he was or what he did?"

Howard replied, "Not a clue. He mysteriously disappeared and then just as mysteriously reappeared. If his staff knows anything, they're not talking. We thought he may have been horsenapped by Biosphere X but it doesn't look like it. We're not sure he ever left Earth. Are you going to meet with him?"

"Him or that Colonel Jupiter. I'll have someone from our embassy along to dump a little more officialese in the pot. How's Ocko?"

"Interested in what you're doing plus trying to track down the killer of the Director of our *Pharm and Pharma* division, Llewellyn Llama. Poisoned with botulinum toxin. We'll welcome your help on that one."

"Sounds like a strange one. Busy times! Say G'day to the Bearoness, the Cubs and Mlle Woof."

"Belinda and Mlle Woof are fine. A word of warning, Bruce. The Furballs are captivated by the movie business. McAra Studios. They'll be coming after you to take on a supporting role in their crime spectacular - The Bold Brave Bears. Guess who they are!"

"They're really bitten. They must have really fallen for that Russian Polar and his film factory. Well, we'll see what happens. Where's Chita nowadays?"

"On her way here, as a matter of fact. She's going to be part of *Pharm and Pharma's* experimental meat development program. The whole gang is descending on the Bear's Lair. Join us as soon as you can get anything on the General. We'll send a plane for you."

"Happy to ride on Ocko's dime. What's your opinion on all this, Howard and Marlin?"

"In the words of Fetlock Holmes, Bruce. Not enough data! We think the General disappeared on his own power and came back when his mission was over but we're damned if we know what that was. I doubt he just went on a vacation and I don't think a filly or mare was involved. But with that nutty steed, who can tell? Let's see what you and Ursula can come up with."

"Thanks for providing me with an Ursula. She's a bonzer sheila. We'll find something, won't we, Ursie?"

"That's fair dinkum, Bruce!"

"OK! Keep us posted and we'll do the same."

"No worries! That crazy horse has an ego that's too big for his own good. Cosmic conquest. What a drongo! Ursie and I will get something out of him and his crew. Tell Ocko we'll see him soon. Cheers!"

Chapter Eleven

Here is someone we've all learned to love
She's descending from heaven above.
Yes, it's Chita – Ms. Catt.
And she knows where it's at
She and Maury both fit paw in glove.

Guess who just arrived. The V-22 Osprey settled onto the taxiway outside the hangar and the oversized swing mounted props spun to a stop, Another gift from the grateful government to Octavius for services rendered. The Octavians don't use this aircraft as much as the Ursa Major C-5A, the Ursa Minor helicopter or the Twin Otter but for longer hauls it's a great substitute for choppers. After taking off vertically, its large tilt-rotor propellers rotate for forward motion making it ideal for short take-off and landing conditions. It's fast and it lands vertically in tight spaces. Not as fast as the F15E Strike Eagle or the guided missile sitting in a silo disguised as a pagoda that round out The Great Bear's Air Force but it serves well.

Two White Bengals, Benedict and Galatea Tigris, the Flying Tigers who pilot Octavius' planes and Belinda's SST were at the controls and had taxied the Osprey to the entry of the Bear's Lair. A tawny spotted cat with distinctive black "tears" around her eyes and the longest legs a feline was entitled to have, strutted down the airstairs. Chita was making an entrance. The Cubs rushed out of the mansion and hurtled toward her. "Aunt Chita, Aunt Chita. Hi, Hi!"

The cat folded both of them in a big embrace. "How are my Little Mischiefs?"

"We're great! We're making a movie. The Bold Brave Bears! You have to be in it!"

"Whoa, Whoa! Let me catch my breath."

Belinda and Mlle Woof had arrived and greeted Chita with bear hugs and doggie tail-wags. "How was your flight?"

"That's a strange airplane. You know how I feel about helicopters. This one isn't quite sure what it is. New York to Cincinnati in a hybrid. Wow! Where is the Great Bear?"

"Inside the mansion." said Bel. "As I think you know, we've had a death and a bunch of issues surrounding the *Pharm and Pharma* cultured meat processes - the Best Burger and Best Wurst. Octavius is counting on your help to untangle the problems. Right now, he's setting up a review for tomorrow to determine whether a division wide audit is warranted. As an obligate-carnivore, your input will be critical."

"I'm not particularly comfortable as the experimental obligate-carnivore, thank you very much."

"Please Chita," she said, "We need your help."

"OK Bel. What the hell! I owe you guys a lot. Even that dopey Kodiak you're married to! All right, Maury, you're on. Fill me in."

"There's a good kitty. I've set up a meeting for Octavius tomorrow morning to decide on whether a *Pharm and Pharma* audit is called for. Our team includes Belinda; the Frau and Colonel; Wolford Wolverine; Roger Rottweiler who is UUI's CFO; Octavius; Ursula and now you. And of course, me. The *Pharm and Pharma* group includes their acting director; their chief biologist and process engineer; their marketing director; lawyer; CFO and two Personal assistants."

"That's quite a crowd! Why don't you toss in The Ohio State University Marching Band while you're at it."

"There will be enough sound and fury without band music. Several of the *Pharm and Pharma* team are loudly opposed to the audit as a waste of time and a schedule killer. Expect fireworks!"

"Nothing like a little excitement! Speaking of which, the Cubs attacked me as I was getting off that flying Mixmaster. Are they really going to try to make a movie? The Bold Brave Bears?"

"Well, they're spending their parent's money, lining up cast members, bringing in equipment and trying to get Jane Huang Hau to act as their cinematographer. They've taken over one of the basements here in the mansion as their studio and also have one lined up in the Shetlands at the Polar Paradise. Does that give you a hint?"

"And you're aiding and abetting all this?"

"Belinda and Octavius think they'll get tired of it shortly before they run through too much cash and credit."

"But you're not so sure."

"I'm never sure of anything with those two. Anyway, Llewellyn's demise is my number one priority with the 'cultured' meat project a close second. The elusive General Turmoil is in third place."

"What's the story with the nutty horse?"

"He disappeared for a couple of weeks and no one, including his own staff, knows where he went. He's back now but no one is any the wiser."

"What's so unusual about that? He's a spook, for God's sake."

"The consensus is something weird is going on."

"Surprise, surprise! I think all horses are crazy, including that Fetlock Holmes."

"I'll withhold judgement on spotted cats."

"Careful, Short Stuff!

"By the way, Bruce Wallaroo is in Washington. He's supposedly representing the Aussie Government to the General's Business on the subject of Multiverse worlds. He's also trying to find out what the General is really doing."

"Lotsa luck, Bruce! He's coming to Cincinnati? I'd like to see him again. Now, let me get myself settled and we can talk some more. I also want to see Octavius."

Not very likely. The Cubs descended on her before she had a chance to step inside. I think Chita was going to have a chance to reprise her performance as a Felonious Feline – a role she played to the hilt. Truth be told, she loved it. Off they headed toward the subterranean studio, each furball hanging on her spotted legs.

I shouted, "Dinner's at seven! Join us for drinks as soon as you extricate yourself."

"I assume the Frau is weaving her gastronomic magic. I hope so. We obligate carnivores do get hungry, even if our consciences bother us. Is she serving 'cultured' meat?"

"Not until the audit starts, if it does. She's supposed to provide Cordon Bleu culinary input. They want you to give the obligate carnivore opinion. *Pharm and Pharma* has run tests and focus groups, of course, but you two have special viewpoints. Meanwhile, watch what commitments you make to the young impresarios. They've gone Hollywood big time."

"Come on, Aunt Chita! We want to show you our studio."

"OK, Bold Brave Bears, but then I have to settle in and go talk with your Momma and Poppa. I'm here to work on the 'cultured' meat project."

McTavish said, "Awww!" and Arabella rolled her eyes. "We need help writing the script. You're a big time magazine publisher. You know how to write. Can't they do without you?"

"In a word, NO! Now come on, show me what you want to show me and then maybe we'll get together in my spare time, if I have any."

"Yes!!" *(Fist bumps.)*

They disappeared into the bowels of the mansion. I headed off to consult with Otto, Condo, Howard and Marlin. They weren't going to be at tomorrow's meeting but I wanted to get their thoughts on Llewellyn's death. I brought Ursula along as well. All the brainpower and experience I could lay my paws on.

We descended on the bar. Marlin joined us from his tank over one of the mansion's closed circuit hookups. Belinda sauntered in fortified with her customary glass of champagne. "Tavi will join us shortly. Better get a keg of mead ready, Maury."

Chapter Twelve

The Octavians all want to know
Who delivered the fatal death blow.
Though Llewellyn is gone
Cultured meat carries on
With Octavius running the show.

The Brain Trust was getting itself lubricated. Frau Ilse was doing her magic in the kitchens but the Colonel arrived to represent the Lupine contingent. Octavius wandered in searching for a measure of mead.

He looked at me. "Did Chita arrive?'

"She did and was promptly captured by the Cubs. They want her full participation in The Bold Brave Bears."

"Bel, I think we have to inject a little reality into that situation. I don't mind a little amateur filmmaking but they're going off the deep end. They want to completely reproduce a Preston Pavel Polar extravaganza. Not only is that expensive. It's impossible and it's going to be damned disruptive. They need to be told the facts of life."

Belinda chuckled and raised an eyebrow. "Good, you do it. Let me know how it turns out." Laughs all around! The Great Bear was not amused.

"All right! Let's concentrate on the issue of Llewellyn. The consensus is that although he died in a Washington hotel room, his death was triggered by person or persons unknown here at *Pharm and Pharma*. Are we agreed on that much?

Since they weren't going to be parties to the great audit debate, Howard, Marlin, Otto and Condo instead had taken up the issue of the botulinum toxin. Howard said "Marlin and I've done some research and developed a theory on Llewellyn's death. As you know he was Type 2 diabetic and suffered from severe neuropathic pain. Isn't that true, Victoria?

78

"Yes, Doctor Watt. There were times when he was in major distress. I wished I could have helped him but he would just grit his teeth and carry on."

Marlin tossed the group a shocker. "We think his death was self-inflicted."

Octavius snorted, "Nonsense! Llewellyn would not commit suicide!"

"I didn't say he did. I think he was doing some self-administered medication using a botox derivative to head off the pain and he miscalculated the effects. There have been some very helpful experiments treating diabetic suffering with botulinum toxin but the results and side effects are not yet fully known and dosages must be very carefully managed. Llewellyn was a scientific and nutritional administrator, not a physician. We suspect he believed he knew enough about the subject to treat himself when the pain got unbearable. He was wrong."

"You're saying his death was accidental?"

"Yes, brought on over a sustained period by overly large doses of the toxin. Insulin doesn't work on Type 2 Diabetes. We were assuming someone malicious inserted the high dosage."

"Not so. He injected himself with dosages of clostridium botulinum packaged to look like insulin to control his neuropathy."

"How do we prove that?"

"For one thing, there was no insulin in his system. Those shots he was taking may have been packaged to look like insulin but they were toxic botulinum."

"But why would he do that?"

"With the Best Wurst and Best Burger projects in play, the last thing he wanted was even the hint of botulism anywhere near the processes. So he fabricated the fake insulin packages to cover his tracks. But, of course, insulin didn't work with Type 2. Very few would suspect, including government inspectors he was using botulinum. Now, that evidence is going to come to the surface."

"Well, like it or not, it looks like Llewellyn unintentionally created the appearance of a potentially serious contamination unless we can prove that he had no access to the experimental food samples. Unfortunately, that's going to be a tough call and the burden of proof is on us. Howard and Marlin, What's your confidence level on your theory?"

"Very high unless you absolutely insist on pinning a murder rap on a *Pharm and Pharma* employee or rival."

The Great Bear frowned. "We need to put this on the front burner at the audit meeting first thing in the morning. We'll have to get Rachel Raccoon, Paul Possum and Jacques Jackrabbit in the picture immediately. They need to prove that all the samples, equipment, venues and individuals are all toxin free. That's a hefty assignment. I hate to disappoint her but I'm not sure I'm up for digging into Frau Schuylkill's feast right now."

Not much of a show of confidence. Howard grinned. "I don't know about you but I'm hungry. It takes more than one meal to do any harm. Llewellyn was at it for quite a while."

Otto, who had been taking all this in, agreed. "What's a little botulism among friends? Let's eat!"

It turned out the Cubs were cadging tastes in the kitchen to the dismay of Mlle Woof, not because of the possible threat to their health but their terrible table manners and insistent gorging. Bold, Brave and Bumptious Bears.

Condo had been quiet up to this point. "Ursula, Did the DC coroner confirm the absence of insulin in Llewellyn's body?"

"His report makes no mention of it. The Director clearly had been injected with the Clostridium Toxin. There was no sign of insulin usage. That's consistent with Type 2 diabetes. I can double check with the coroner but I support Howard's and Marlin's theory. I strongly suspect the

Director lost control of his self-treatment. He must have been in awful pain."

Octavius shook his massive head. "A terrible event. Yes, Ursula! Please do check and then we'll get onto the Washington Police. Let's also query Llewellyn's brother. See what he knows about the Director's condition. Meanwhile, let's get ready for tomorrow's discussion. It isn't going to be pretty. If we go ahead with the audit, that's going to call for some radical changes in schedules and personnel. We also have to think about naming Llewellyn's replacement. I want to leave Jacques in charge of the development and manufacturing processes. Our Mr. Inside. We need a top-notch Mr. Outside. Llewellyn was an excellent diplomat and public relations expert. He was an ideal choice to represent *Pharm and Pharma* to the government, the food industries and all the advocacy groups. Any thoughts on a replacement?"

I interjected. "How about you?"

"Me?"

"Hey, it's your company. And you have the authority, reputation, connections and the smarts. Take over for at least long enough to get through the launch and find a full-time Director at your leisure after a thorough search. But, please can we discuss all this over dinner?"

"All right. Let's not disappoint the Frau."

Freed by the Cubs, Chita sauntered in, a bowl of champagne in her paws. "Greetings all!"

"Hello Chita! Off on another cinematic venture? Maury, while you're eating, bring Ms. Catt up to speed on the situation and the personalities involved."

"If we're going to discuss Rachel Raccoon, I'm going to need another drink. Nothin' like a shot of fermented coconut milk VSOP to smooth out the kinks."

The Bear picked up his oversized smartphone and called the acting Director. "Jacques? Octavius! I wanted to call you before tomorrow morning's session. Look! We have concluded that Llewellyn's death was an accident. An overdose of a botulinum derivative to alleviate extreme pain. I'll explain it more fully in the morning. Second, I have decided to take over his job until the launch is complete. No reflection on you. Quite the contrary. With your talents, knowledge and experience I want you controlling the process full time to completion. I'm going to play the part of Mr. Outside. I have plenty of history in managing relationships and smoothing out bumps especially where the government is concerned. I'll announce that tomorrow, too. I suspect you're relieved. Get some sleep. I'll see you in the AM."

Chapter Thirteen

It's a loss for Ms. Rachel Raccoon
Who had argued the whole afternoon.
Her resistance fell through.
There will be a review.
The audit commences quite soon.

Next morning, we contacted the Washington coroner and police. They confirmed that Llewellyn had not been taking insulin and bought our theory of a botulinum overdose. Lewis Lama told us his brother had been battling neuropathic pain for quite some time and had experimented with a range of remedies, including botox and other botulinum derivatives. Sorry as we all were at what befell Llewellyn, there was a feeling of relief that we were not in pursuit of a murderer. We couldn't absolutely prove an accident but it seemed to be the most logical conclusion. Everyone involved accepted it as the most likely scenario.

Later in the morning, our entourage headed from the Bear's Lair across the river to a large conference room at UUI. It's time for our session with *Pharm and Pharma* management to discuss the need for an audit of the Best Burger and Best Wurst programs. All told the players were a formidable group. Our team includes Belinda; the Frau and Colonel; Wolford Wolverine; Roger Rottweiler who is UUI's CFO; Ursula; Chita and me. And of course, Octavius.

The *Pharm and Pharma* group was represented by their technical director, Jacques Jackrabbit; their chief biologist, Rachel Raccoon; Paul Possum, head process engineer; Roland Reynard, resident chef; Ormand Oryx, their marketing director; Serena Serval, their lawyer; the *P&P* CFO, a Chinstrap Penguin named Clarence and the two executive personal assistants. Also represented were scientists from three nutritional testing labs from leading universities, none of whom had been working with *P&P* in the past. (*If there was to be an audit, we wanted no tainted or biased results!*)

Before Octavius could even call the meeting to order, Rachel Raccoon was on her hind legs protesting in strident terms against the need for an in-depth review. The Bear drew himself up to his full nine feet, stared at her as only he could stare and said, "Ms. Raccoon, I am chairing this meeting. I welcome your comments and reactions but at the appropriate time. Right now, I have a few announcements I need to make."

That didn't shut her down. "Ms. Raccoon, you're an extremely valuable employee but not irreplaceable. May I suggest that you refrain from any more outbursts and hold your opinions till you are called upon. You will be given ample opportunity to express yourself."

She shook her head in frustration and flopped down in her seat. I don't think I have ever seen a Raccoon pout before. She hissed at Paul Possum, her erstwhile ally in seeking to derail the audit. He shrugged and she threw her paws in the air.

"All right," said Octavius, "Let's proceed. I've spoken to Doctor Jackrabbit and he is aware of what I am about to say."

"First, we strongly believe Doctor Lama was the victim of an accidental overdose of a botulinum derivative he had been taking to counteract extreme pain brought about by Type 2 Diabetes. We think that mystery has been solved. If any of you have any information that could prove contrary, please see me immediately after this meeting."

"Now. commencing immediately I have somewhat reluctantly agreed to fill in for Llewellyn for the duration of this project or until an outstanding new Director can be found for *Pharm and Pharma*. I am rearranging my rather overloaded schedule in order to carry this out and I would like Victoria Vicuna to help me as my Personal Assistant. *(She eagerly nodded.)* Because he is so essential to the cultured meat program, I have asked Jacques Jackrabbit to resume his original assignment full-time and he has agreed."

Have you ever seen a raging Raccoon? Rachel, diplomat extraordinaire, was once more on her feet. "But you don't know anything about this project. Besides taking up time with this stupid audit, we're going to have to undergo immense delays and expend unnecessary effort keeping you on track. This is just too much."

"Ms. Raccoon, much as I would hate to see it happen, we can arrange for you to leave the project and *Pharm and Pharma*, if you so desire. Please remember that you are bound by stringent non-disclosure and non-compete agreements which I assure you we will enforce to the fullest. Isn't that so, Serena and Wolford?"

Both lawyers reluctantly nodded their heads. Wolford looked at the Raccoon and said, "I can assure you, Rachel. Doctor Bear, does not make idle threats even if they might have a negative effect on the Best Wurst and Best Burger projects or any of his other business ventures or assets. I'm sure your departure will be unwelcome but please remember that this program and indeed, all of *Pharm and Pharma* are extremely small elements in the UUI corporate empire. Elements that have great potential but are hardly earth shattering at the moment. *(Jacques looked horrified.)* May I suggest we all take a few deep breaths, settle back and allow the day to progress. If, at the conclusion, you wish to exercise your option to leave, we can make the appropriate arrangements."

I could see Serena staring at Rachel and mouthing, "Don't be a jerk!" Paul Possum was also giving her non-verbal cues to calm down.

The Raccoon frowned but sat back down and wonder of wonders, shut up! I was wondering what was driving her belligerence. What would the audit uncover? Were there some serious nasty issues she and the process engineer didn't want to come to the surface? I even flirted with revisiting Llewellyn's death. Suppose it really wasn't an accident. Maury the paranoid! I needed some time with Ursula tout suite. As I looked at our team, I could tell similar ideas were forming in their minds. This was going to be more than a simple business inquiry.

Octavius deferred to the two CFO's and lawyer who had first suggested an audit. Clarence Chinstrap, Serena Serval and Roger Rottweiler. The dog from UUI led off. He booted up a computer app on a wide screen and said, "Clarence, Serena and I cooperated to put this recommendation together. As we told you at our last meeting, *Pharm and*

Pharma has several very profitable product and service lines and is in good financial condition. Our outside accounting firm has recently attested to that fact. That is not the object of our suggested audit."

"We want to validate the feasibility of the cultured meat venture and its offerings. Are the products top quality? Is our marketing program on target, convincing and effective? What about support and distribution; safety; insurability and social acceptance? Will the government approve? Most of all, will our customers want to eat the stuff? Can we sell enough to justify the effort and expense? This is food, after all. Can we capture a meaningful part of the global market?"

Paul Possum interrupted, "We've handled all of that. Why go over it again?"

Serena responded. "Because **_WE'VE_** handled all that. We need objective assurances by an experienced outside entity that the program is and will continue to be viable."

Rachel shouted, "We'll lose our competitive edge if we wait on this!"

Clarence shook his black and white head. "Do we really have a competitive edge? How do we know?"

Jacques looked at them and asked, "Who are these experienced outside entities who will give us warm and fuzzy feelings?"

Roger waved into the audience. "We have invited bids from consultants from three research labs and business schools to collaborate on this project. Doctor Bear, we are hoping you will lead the selection process and act as their client,"

Octavius looked around the room. "OK, but I am assuming we can reach satisfactory conclusions within ninety days."

The Colonel and Howard both raised their eyebrows. "That's a very short time frame."

The Bear responded. "That's what these bidders are going to have to confirm. Most of the technical and business data already exists and we've already done marketing studies. This will mostly be an exercise in revalidation. We'll take the bids shortly."

"As far as the actual products are concerned, I've asked Ms. Catherine Catt, or Chita as she prefers to be called, to act as an objective Obligate Carnivore test subject. Chita has a very discerning palate and as a media editor/publisher, is not afraid to frankly express her opinions. Frau Ilse Schuylkill, a Cordon Bleu chef, has agreed to manage a test kitchen for the products. If the results are as successful as I hope they will be, we will have excellent marketing content and suggestions. A satisfied publisher and a world famous cook. If not, I think we know the way back to the drawing boards. It looks like the audit is a go. Any comments before we begin the interviews?"

That was Rachel's chance but I think she realized good jobs for food biologists weren't that easy to come by. With a toss of her head, she stood and left the room. Paul scurried out after her. Ormand Oryx and Jacques Jackrabbit came forward to participate in the interviews.

Belinda walked up to Octavius, Wolford and me. "Expect some intense passive resistance from the raccoon and possum."

Wolford shook his head. "Perhaps I should have another private conversation with the two of them. The last thing we need is some guerilla warfare, pardon the pun."

I scratched my nose. "There's something wrong here. A ninety day delay is something you get used to in major projects. They're overreacting. I believe they may have something to hide. What do you think, Ursula?"

The AGI said, "You may be right, Maury. Do you have any problem if I do some independent investigation, Doctor Bear?"

"Not at all, Ursula, but first let's get with Jacques…or do you suppose he might be part of the problem."

Belinda said, "Let's assume he's not and see what he has to say by way of explaining Rachel and Paul's antagonism. It will give us additional insight into his management style and involvement. Maury, we could use

Otto and Condo on a follow up tomorrow. Nobody suspects a goofy otter or a voice-throwing condor."

I chuckled, "Little do they know."

Octavius called Jacques, "Before you join the interview committee, let's chat for a minute."

The Jackrabbit hopped over to join us.

"Can you justify this hostility of Rachel and Paul?"

"They have been working extra-long days and hours and have applied some real genius to the project. Rachel is a top notch biologist and has made some really remarkable contributions to the science. Paul and his team have developed some truly innovative techniques for artificially reproducing protein and animal cells in bulk. The processes scale up dramatically. You can understand their frustration at more delays and at having their work once again questioned."

"I sympathize but those are the facts of life. None of the programs at UUI have gone as smoothly as we'd like and this one could affect lives. It's high risk. I don't want anyone even getting an upset stomach from Best Wurst or Best Burgers. *(I'm still not sure I like those names.)* If something dire should happen once the products are in the marketplace, it could mean the end of *P&P*, UUI, personal bankruptcy, lawsuits and even criminal proceedings. This voluntary audit isn't going to totally buffer us but it may result in a few important catches and keep us from making several dangerous, costly or stupid mistakes. Plus it shows how conscientious we are about quality and safety. No, we're going to do this and Rachel and Paul have to be energetically on board. Wolford, I'm going to join you when you talk with them. Jacques, in spite of how you may feel personally, I expect you to be enthusiastic about this review."

*****

The vendor interviews went smoothly and the contract was given to a partnership of two consulting firms who had biology trained staffs engaged in nutrition measurement and diet packaging. One group specialized in Obligate Carnivore requirements. They were ready to begin work immediately once contracts were signed and principals were vetted.

*****

Wolford had tracked down Rachel and Paul and was using his Wolverine persuasiveness to bring them around to cooperation with the program. Octavius, the Frau, Chita and I joined them as did Ursula operating in silent, passive, observer mode. Most members of UUI and its subsidiaries were unaware of the Artificial General Intelligence system. To most of them, she was just a laptop computer. That's the way we wanted it.

Serena joined the group. Paul was the first to surrender. "I suppose, in the long run, this will further validate what we've been doing, Rachel. We'll be making progress. We still have a hefty agenda to carry out while this review is going on."

The raccoon reluctantly agreed. "Keep their interference to a minimum. We need to keep moving forward."

Octavius nodded. "Toward that end, I want you to meet two individuals who I hope will be major supports for you. I know you already have an elaborate test kitchen and taste specialists on staff. However, Frau Ilse Schuylkill is a first class, Cordon Bleu chef who has been with me for years and has delighted the rich, powerful and famous with her culinary wizardry. I have asked her to apply her imagination to creating delectable dishes based on Best Wurst and Best Burgers. Her reputation alone will dramatically enhance the products' images and I'm sure her suggestions will serve to create even more desirable results.

My spotted and long-legged colleague (!) here, Madame Catherine Catt, *(Chita to her friends,)* is a famous publisher and social media leader for the worldwide feline community. She is also an Obligate Carnivore. She will be evaluating both Frau Schuylkill's productions and the output from your test kitchens and disseminating the results in her publications and electronic outlets.

Chita snuffled. "Don't worry. I'll discuss it with you first. Favorable reactions from an Obligate should go a long way to promote Best Wurst and Burgers. Let's get to it."

The Development of Civilization Volume Eleven - Part Four

Food, Drink and the Senses

(From "An Introduction to Faunapology" by Octavius Bear Ph.D.)

Most animals have five basic senses: touch, sight, hearing, smell and taste. The organs associated with each sense send information to the brain to help us recognize and understand our surroundings. In addition to the basic five, there are other senses such as balance, gravity, pain, self-awareness and hunger. Individuals may have sensory abilities that vary by species. This discussion will concentrate on those perceptions that involve food and drink. To a lesser or greater degree, these involve the five basic senses plus hunger. They are the key determinants of how pleasurable a specific eating or drinking experience will be and how successfully a particular food or beverage will fare in the world at large. They are crucial to our project.

In working to achieve acceptance of "cultured meat," developers must aim for a combination of sensations that appeal to the broadest number of consumer types.

These include touch, especially the sensation of "mouth feel." Most mammals have a strong preference for a substantial texture typical of natural meat. There is a need in some cases to attach the meat component to an edible "pseudo-bone" in order for it to be truly satisfying.

Sight-What does the cultured meat look like? In the animal kingdom, this presents some unique problems since not all animals see alike. Some are color blind. Some see in ultra-violet or infra-red. Certain colors are unpleasant or threatening. Any "cultured meat" offering must come in a variety of colors, shapes and sizes.

Hearing-This may not seem to be as important as the other senses in determining the success of "artificial meat." Consider the sizzle of a cooked burger or steak. The crunch of a bone.

*Smell -This sense combines with taste to form the critical yes-no for a lab produced edible substance. Obviously, not all odors are equally appealing to all animals even if we restrict the universe to Obligate Carnivores. It has also been demonstrated that the senses of smell and taste often merge to create a single, complex gustatory sensation. **Flavor!** This may also be enhanced by the application of heat and of liquids such as gravies or broths.*

*Now we come to the sensory deal breaker – **Taste**. A composite and convoluted sense, taste itself is usually characterized as having five basic aspects: sweet, bitter, sour, salty and umami.*

Sweetness, often but not always regarded as a pleasurable sensation, is produced by the presence of sugars and several other substances. Most animals enjoy it but not necessarily in meat.

Bitterness is a sharp feeling and ranges from the enjoyable to the off-putting. Often found in drinks and the juice of fruits, it is frequently characterized as an "acquired taste." Once again, its applicability to meat is limited.

Sourness is an acidic sensation caused by hydrogen ions and can be a taste problem. There are exceptions like pickles which appeal to many mammals and are often paired with meat as a side dish.

Saltiness is the taste characteristic of sodium chloride, an essential in proper amounts for bodily health. Witness "salt licks" as popular gathering spots for animals. However, too much sodium can be dangerous as well as unpleasant.

Umami. The word is Japanese and means savory taste. It is characteristic of broths and cooked meats and is important to producing enjoyable prepared cultured meat.

Combine all these characteristics with supplying basic nourishment and responding to an animal's digestive demands and you can get an appreciation for the challenges faced by Pharm and Pharma developers in creating Best Burgers and Best Wurst. These substances will no doubt begin life as novelties or dietary supplements and, if successful, then progress to mainstream and eventually dominant status. Social and political pressure as well as resistance by the conventional food industries will bear heavily on producing acceptance or failure. The issue of consumer cost is paramount.

In short, this is no trivial exercise and our additional audit is warranted in spite of the care that has already been exerted in bringing "cultured meat" to the worldwide market. We shall see.

Chapter Fourteen

So General Turmoil has wed
A beautiful tall thoroughbred.
She's won races, it's true.
She's a scientist too
And a quite wealthy mare, so it's said

With the audit off and running, we returned to the Bear's Lair for a little R&R and joint discussion. Before we could get through a round of late afternoon refreshment, Ursula rang her chime. "I have the Chief Inspector on the line from Washington. He has an Ursula copy on his laptop. Here he is."

"Thanks Ursie! G'day all! Greetings from your nation's capital. I have news. First off, the Business and the Australian Inter-Cosmos Authority have established a cooperative initiative for joint exploration of alternate universes. *(Courtesy of me and General Turmoil.)* I'm looking to involve you folks as consultants to Oz Land. I'm planning to run up there tomorrow to Cincinnati to discuss it further with you."

Frau Schuylkill groaned. The Inspector invariably created havoc throughout the mansion with his jumping and bouncing around.

Octavius snorted. "That's an interesting development. We'll want to investigate it with you in some detail before signing on. But you mentioned General Turmoil. Is he back in town after his mysterious disappearance? Where was he?"

The Wallaroo guffawed. "The Great Secret has been unraveled! You won't believe it. No dangerous or clandestine plot. No capture by hostile baddies. The General got married! He was off on a secret honeymoon."

The shocked looks rippled around the room. I had trouble controlling a laugh. The idea of that iron-tailed equine having a romantic side was beyond belief. Or perhaps it was a marriage of convenience or necessity.

Belinda broke the ice. "Who is the *(un)* lucky female?"

Bruce, who was holding in his own laughter, replied. "A thoroughbred mare named Quantum Lady. She is famous in equestrian circles for her looks, intelligence and speed. She is independently wealthy and considered quite a catch. She is a university graduate with advanced degrees in physics and astrobiology. They met at a scientific conference and things proceeded from there."

I asked. "Will she be joining the Business?"

"Not clear but it certainly seems likely. I doubt if she is taken up with domesticity, society doings or the track although they say she has won several major races. You may want to make her acquaintance, Bearoness. It sounds like you two Sheilas may have a lot in common."

Howard, whose feelings for the General certainly ran to the negative, shook his head and said, "I've heard of her. She's written a few worthwhile articles on quantum physics. I don't know which came first, her name or her avocation. She could be an interesting player in the Business' programs. Of course, she'd have to get clearances and scientific vetting but I doubt if she'd have that much trouble. I agree with the Chief Inspector, Bearoness. A congratulatory call might be in order. What do you think, Octavius?"

"That's up to Belinda. It would make for a fascinating association."

Bel paused for a moment and then said, "What the Hell. Why not? But I think Chita and the Frau ought to join me. It might actually change our relationship with the Business and even the General himself, although that may be pushing credibility too far. Let's see if we get accepted or snubbed. We could offer to fly her up to Cincinnati or join her in Washington. Where are they living, Bruce?"

"Somewhere in the Virginia horse country although the General will certainly keep his DC quarters as well. I'll get you her address. This should be interesting."

*****

95

The UUI heavy duty helicopter settled in on a broad grass expanse in Middleburg, Virginia. In the background a large, white colonial mansion stood at the end of a tree-lined roadway - the home of the thoroughbred mare, formerly known as Quantum Lady. In the foreground, standing at attention with her head and tail erect was a gorgeous, stately Chestnut watching the aircraft's descent and landing. Dressed in a dark red satin blanket, she exuded dignity and self-confidence. Standing by her side next to a large travel case was a smaller roan mare in black livery-no doubt her maid.

Belinda cut the engines, lowered the cargo ramp and emerged to greet her guest-passenger. "Mrs. Turmoil, I am Bearoness Belinda Béarnaise Bruin Bear *(nee Black)*- Known as Bel or Mrs. Octavius Bear. What a pleasure to meet you. Congratulations on your recent marriage. Such a lovely estate. I assume it is yours. Is the General in Washington? *(Affirmative head nod to both.)* We're so happy you agreed to join us for a few days in Cincinnati."

"I normally pilot our aircraft when I travel to keep my skills and certifications up to date. This morning, you will be flown back to southwest Ohio by our White Bengal twins, Benedict and Galatea Tigris, or as we call them, The Flying Tigers. Let me introduce you."

Ben and Gal had been sitting in the cargo bay and rose to greet the horses who were taken aback by the pure white pelts of the two felines. The Chestnut exclaimed, "My goodness! Aren't the three of you all lovely in sparkling white - and skilled aviators, too. I am indeed impressed. Let me introduce my maid, Clarissa. *(Mutual bows.)* My name is Lucinda, nee Caballa. I am still not used to being called Mrs. Turmoil and Quantum Lady was my racing moniker. I don't use it anymore although I still enjoy quantum physics and astrobiology."

Belinda smiled and said, "You're hardly deficient in the beauty department or the sciences. You have a great reputation. I can see why the General finds you so attractive." Looking past them into the helicopter's fuselage, she waved at two fur covered meteors. "These are Octavius' and my twin cubs – Arabella and McTavish. They pleaded to come along for the ride. Be grateful for the noise of the chopper's engines or they will talk your ears off."

Not to be put off, the Cubs ran up to Lucinda and shouted, "Hi, Mrs. General. We're Arabella and McTavish. Pointing at the breathless Bichon Frisé. This is our governess, Mlle Woof. We're also twins. We make movies. Would you like a part in our next film? The Bold Brave Bears - that's us. We know a Horse. Fetlock Holmes. He's a famous detective. Our Poppa is a famous detective, too. He's also a typhoon."

"I think you mean tycoon, dear."

"That's what I said."

Bel interrupted. "All right you two. Get seated. Lucinda and Clarissa have to get on board with their luggage and we're starting up the engines."

Lucinda looked at Belinda. "They are so charming. I didn't realize Polar Bears and Kodiaks could have offspring."

"On very rare occasions. They are pretty unusual. Charming is not the word I would use to describe them although I am a proud mother. I'm afraid this ride is going to be noisy but we'll have lots of time to chat and compare notes when we arrive at the mansion. We have a very talented and unusual organization who are all looking forward to greeting you. That includes several scientists who are anxious to be introduced."

The Horse responded, "I've never been to Cincinnati but I am familiar with Doctor Bear and UUI as well as Doctor Howard Watt and his associate Marlin. Some of their publications are fascinating. I'm awaiting the opportunity to meet them as well. As far as the Business is concerned, I hope to be able to participate in Reginald's programs. *(Reginald?)* But military bureaucracy being what it is, I have to go through all sorts of reviews and vetting and clearances before I can do anything useful. I really welcome the chance to meet and perhaps even collaborate with fellow scientists, especially on the subject of alternate universes. I'm sure you folks have your confidentiality requirements but we can certainly work within them."

Belinda wondered what that might involve. A bit of care was going to be necessary. She needed to talk with Octavius as well as Howard and Marlin. She said, "Oh, We have a stop to make in Washington. We're picking up Chief Inspector Wallaroo from Australia. He's joining us at the Bear's Lair. I think you've met him. He's quite a character."

Galatea took that moment to give take-off instructions and the engines started their loud acceleration. On to the Queen City and its environs.

Chapter Fifteen

Our Frau Schuylkill is wearing a frown.
Since Bruce Wallaroo's coming to town.
Every time he arrives,
She breaks out with fierce hives
And approaches a nervous breakdown.

In *P&P's* experimental kitchens, Frau Ilse Schuylkill was laying down the law with Ormand Oryx and his marketeers; Roland Reynard, resident chef; several sous-chefs and short order cooks. Chita looked on, an amused smile on her spotted face,

"Ach, Herr Reynard and Oryx, if we are to make Best Wurst and Best Burgers really attractive, we must use some culinary and marketing ingenuity. Do they really look like delicious meats? What about color and texture? What can we do here in the kitchen to make them look their best? How can we enhance the smells? What spices should we add? Have you been working on sauces? Mustards? Chilis? Let's think combinations. Let's think complete meals. Let's think wine, beers. Vegetables! We must improve the mouth feel through cookery. Come, Roland. We must invent soups. What kind of bread will make the Best Wurst and Burger sandwiches? We have to give the meat the ideal settings to show off its best qualities. Grilling and barbeque! Variety, variety! From five star restaurants to road side hash houses!!"

"Ms. Chita here is a true gourmet and an Obligate Carnivore. Let's cater to her taste buds. Give her something to write, publish and fill her websites with.

Chita chimed in. "I want to stage a 'cultured meat' event with world famous chefs competing for prizes. Let's produce wurst and burger celebrations like Ocktoberfests in major cities here and overseas. We need renowned luminaries to act as Best Meat representatives. Endorsements from the Rich and Famous; Athletes; Show Biz types; Medical Specialists; Tastemakers; Obligate Carnivores; Animal Rights Advocates;

Academics; Dieticians and Weight Watchers; Teenagers. Get Octavius' and Belinda's Cubs involved. Everyone loves cute."

Ormand Oryx sucked in his breath. "Will Doctor Bear really go for that kind of expense?"

"Octavius is rich beyond belief. He'll finance it. Trust me."

The Culinary Fox looked down his pointed nose at Ilse. "We are not complete incompetents in these kitchens, Frau Schuylkill. We have been waiting for management to give us the go-ahead to begin our programs after we get government approval."

"I apologize, Herr Reynard. My enthusiasm often runs away with me when it comes to food. But let us join paws and begin the experimental programs now. We can't wait forever for the government. We should be ready to reach out and move. It may stir up the bureaucrats. If Chita and Ormand can secure their celebrity representatives to act as our test subjects, we can have these kitchens really humming. We will make mistakes but we will also produce sumptuous results if the meats are as good as I believe they are. Of course, you are in charge."

Somewhat mollified, Reynard smiled. "You have certainly outlined a number of areas we have not yet pursued. Let's lay out a development plan and menus and get these sous-chefs and cooks busy. We'll need to re-check the kitchens and equipment and make assignments. But the first thing we need is an adequate, consistent and steady supply of meat to work with. I'll get on Paul Possum. He and Rachel are still experimenting and maybe we can give them some direction and inducement. He needs to get his production facilities running at higher speed. Perhaps, Ms. Chita, you can also do a feature on the process itself. Interview Rachel Raccoon and Paul Possum without giving away any secrets. That should also give them some more incentive while this audit is going on. Don't forget Jacques and us."

The cat chirped, "Already working on it, Rollo. You're at the top of my Quiz List. I've ordered up a camera crew; a couple of scriptwriters; musicians and narrators.

100

She turned to Ilse. "I'll have to keep the Cubs under control. They'll want to stick their little black noses into producing the shows. But I do want them as endorsers. I'll have to talk with Belinda."

"All right," said the Frau, "Shall we meet tomorrow, Roland? Chita, do you and Ormand want to work separately and then we can get together in a couple of days, compare notes and report to Octavius and Jacques."

Agreement all around.

"Meanwhile," said the Cat, "Bruce is on his way up here from Washington and I gather we have a special guest coming as well – General Turmoil's new wife and her maid. Belinda, the Flying Tigers and the Cubs have both of them ensconced in a large UUI helicopter. This should be fascinating. I would never have predicted this event."

Ilse frowned. "The Bouncing Bobby is coming? I'd better get over to the mansion and protect the furniture and breakables. What do we know about the general's wife.?

"Not much except she's a beautiful, brilliant horse who's up on Quantum theory. Octavius and Belinda want to meet her as do Howard and Marlin. I'm not sure we should trust her."

"You're beginning to sound like me, Chita. Suspicious, suspicious, suspicious!

"I learned that from the Deadly Duck. Hmm! I hadn't though much about him since I killed him. *(See Book Five – The Curse of the Mummy's Case)*

"Let's go back to the Bear's Lair and go on preservation duty."

Chapter Sixteen

The two horses have come all this way.
Just how long are they planning to stay?
Bruce is wary at best
And he's really hard pressed
To explain what strange game is in play.

"Watch the ragin' rotors, young ones." This from Chief Inspector Bruce Wallaroo of the Australian International Police *(on Special Multiverse Negotiation Assignment to the US-based agency, The Business.)* He was talking to the Cubs. Readers of earlier Casebook stories know that Bruce is a unique, nay bizarre, helicopter pilot himself who flies the way he ambles on the ground – with swoops, leaps, bounces, jumps and hops. This time he was a passenger on a UUI heavy duty chopper under the control of Ben and Gal Tigris with Belinda, the Cubs, Mlle Woof, Lucinda Turmoil and her maid, Clarissa. He was enjoying the stately progression not at all.

As the Flying Tigers brought the whirlybird to a sedate halt near the oversized hangar in the Bear's Lair's extensive courtyard, the Cubs had tossed off their seatbelts and rushed to the cargo door. "Open up, Ben! Let us out, Gal! We have to show Mrs. General around."

Belinda ordered them back to their seats and Mlle Woof stared them down. "You wait till it's safe, mes petits. We don't want chopped bear cubs for dinner!"

This resulted in gales of hysterical laughter from the meteoric furballs who perfectly matched Bruce's bursts of dramatic speed. Lucinda whickered and shook her head at the "bearlets" who had been trying to caper and shout above the noise of the engines all the way from Washington. She looked at Belinda and said, "Have you determined how to package all that energy? You could supply enough power to fuel the entire countryside."

"They'd have to stand still long enough for us to hook them up. By the way, their current passion is movie-making. Don't let them persuade you to take a role in their latest spectacular – The Bold Brave Bears."

"That sounds fascinating. Maybe Clarissa would like a shot at stardom."

The roan snorted and bobbed her head. Not clear whether that was a "yes, a no" or an embarrassed hiccup.

The cargo door opened and Octavius proceeded up the ramp, almost trampling the hurtling Cubs as they raced out. "Mrs. Turmoil, welcome to the Bear's Lair. We're happy to have you with us. I must admit your visit is quite unexpected but then the Bearoness can be quite persuasive."

"No persuasion was necessary, Doctor Bear. I have been an admirer of you and your colleagues for quite some time. I am looking forward to meeting them and spending time with you. Thank you for your gracious welcome."

"Well, we'll let you get settled in and then go through the introductions. Here is Frau Ilse Schuylkill, our estate manager/chief pilot/Cordon Bleu chef/security officer along with her mate, Colonel Wyatt Where. I should also warn you *(Chuckle, chuckle)* They're formidable sharpshooters."

"Good afternoon, Madame Turmoil. Welcome. No fear from firearms. My mate and I have been retired from the military for quite some time. We have rooms set aside for you and your companion. Please follow me. One of our domestics will see to your luggage. I have a luncheon set on when you are ready. Doctor Bear, The Bearoness and several of their associates will be joining us. Hello, Inspector. We have rooms for you, too."

Octavius shook Bruce's paw. "Welcome, Bruce! Good to see you again. We have lots to talk about. Get settled and join us for lunch and a beer."

"G'day Ocko! Yer lookin' yer splendid self. I could use a cold one. Just be a jiffy and I'll join yer."

At the mention of food, the Cubs scampered off to the kitchens with Mlle Woof in hot pursuit. The Flying Tigers joined them for a quick lunch before returning the helicopter to UUI.

When Bruce returned and got his paw around a tinny, Octavius asked. "What do you think of our guests?"

"There's somethin' wrong there, chief!"

"How do you mean?"

"She sat in on several of our meetins' at the Business and the General acted as if she was in charge."

"Wives can be like that. Look at Belinda."

"Not the same! This one is runnin' the show. I'm not even sure they're married. She may be the Boss and he's workin' fer her. Be careful what she's doin'. I think she's on a spy mission."

The Bear summoned Ursula. He asked the AGI to follow up on the General's marriage and ferret out Lucinda's background and history.

At that moment, the Horses entered the huge, ornate dining room.

"This is a spectacular building, Doctor Bear. We are both very much impressed, aren't we Clarissa?"

"Oh yes. I thought our mansion was exciting but this is exceptional. I understand you have a large laboratory and workshop in the basement. We'd love to see them. Perhaps after lunch?"

A thought rattled through the Bear's brain. *"She doesn't sound like any maid or companion I'm used to. Bruce may well be right. I think I'll get Belinda and the Frau to scout them out. I'll put Chita in the mix as well. Could Clarissa be the Boss Lady?"*

"I guess that can arranged. *(with restrictions)* First, let me introduce my associates whom you haven't met yet."

104

(Ursula, check out Clarissa as well.)

While they were talking, several of the Octavians entered the dining room and took up seats around the table. "Lucinda Turmoil and Clarissa – sorry, I don't know your last name."

"Just plain Mare, Doctor."

"Please call me Octavius. Anyway, Lucinda and Clarissa, may I present Maury Meerkat, my sidekick, number one assistant and aide-de-camp. *(Nods)* You've met the Frau. This is her mate, Colonel Wyatt Where. *(More Nods)* This impressive looking bird is L. Condor, *(Condo to his friends)* a marvelous Brazilian telecommunications specialist and vocal genius, *(A pleasure, Senhora and Senhorita)* Seated on your right is a highly talented Otter who has special mission capabilities *(No mention of Otto's involvement with Multiverse activities.)* This lovely feline is Ms. Catherine Catt, noted publisher and social media maven. Call her Chita."

(So far, the reaction was casual politesse. Here comes the main event.) Now let me acquaint you in the flesh with two individuals you are familiar with through their publications - Doctor Howard Watt; our brilliant Porcupine scientist and technologist; laser and weapons specialist; Multiverse expert and Quantum Mechanics genius and Marlin, a Dolphin and the Prince of Whales' Chief Scientist who works closely with Howard."

Bells rang. Both Lucinda and Clarissa sat up and stared at the two professionals. Lucinda whinnied. "I am so glad to finally make your acquaintance, gentlebeasts. We *(WE?)* look forward to spending time conferring with you on Multiverse matters. Hopefully, you can make yourselves available to compare notes."

Marlin spoke from his tank over a closed circuit hookup. "Pleased to meet you, ladies. We are engaged in a series of experiments that occupy much of our time but I suppose we can schedule some moments to get together."

Clarissa, who increasingly was shedding her identity as Lucinda's maid, confidante and companion and taking on the role of collaborator and colleague and possible leader, said, "That would be wonderful. We were so hoping to work with you."

That comment set off some serious questions in the Great Bear's mind and among the other players. Ursula was running in silent mode so she couldn't comment at the moment.

"Well," said Octavius, raising an eyebrow, "Now that we're all acquainted, let's dig into the Frau's delicious lunch."

Chapter Seventeen

Has somebody stolen Best Wurst?
Has Best Burger been totally cursed?
Has there been a bad leak?
P&P's not unique?
Are there others who've gotten there first?

The *P&P* audit was well underway and so far, so good. No financial irregularities had surfaced; process and experimental record keeping looked accurate and complete; raw materials were adequately accounted for. Now came the critical attestations. The end products themselves and the validity of the procedures! Rachel, Paul and Jacques were carefully supervising the tests being carried out by the lab assessors, making certain that confidentiality was being preserved according to the Non-Disclosure Agreements. Samples were painstakingly controlled. Roland Reynard and the kitchen staff were called in to prepare trial servings. Frau Schuylkill was in attendance. So was Chita and several professional tasters. The results fit the prescribed specs. Any previous discrepancies caught by Doctors Llewellyn and Jackrabbit seemed to have been ironed out. All good!

However, during a break one of the auditors remarked, "You know, there's a remarkable similarity between meat being developed by Advanced Sustenance and *P&P*. I worked on some early experiments for

Advanced and *P&P* is well ahead. I can't say any more than that without violating confidentiality."

Rachel popped up her head. "What do you mean? We're convinced our processes and products are unique."

"Sorry, I can't say any more. I shouldn't have even said that."

The Raccoon turned to Paul. "Do we have a leak somewhere? Advanced is a two-bit outfit with second raters on their staff. They couldn't have gotten to our level without help. Where's Doctor Bear?"

Octavius trundled over. "Is there a problem?"

Rachel chittered and hissed. "I'll say. One of the inspectors thinks Advanced Sustenance is developing meat very similar to ours. He can't say any more than that. Advanced couldn't have done it on their own. You're a detective. How about you and your staff tracking it down? Just what we need. Industrial Espionage!"

Given Rachel's volatile personality and possessive emotions toward her work, Octavius' first reaction was to write off her suspicions. "But," he thought, "we're doing this review and we can't afford to let anything like this slip by. Maury, Ursula! Dig this out."

Chapter Eighteen

The Octavians have much work to do!
They must deal with a plot if it's true.
Our astute AGI
Says Lucinda's a spy.
And it seems that Clarissa is too.

Let's hear it for Ursula's multi-tasking skills. While she was picking up on the Advanced Sustenance issue for *P&P*, she was also doing searches on Lucinda Turmoil and Clarissa Mare. Who were they, really? Was the Business launching a spying effort on the Bear's Multiverse Projects?

"Maury, I cannot find any record of a marriage between General Reginald Turmoil and Lucinda Caballa and I cannot pinpoint a Clarissa Mare or actually, I found six Clarissa Mares. I don't want to jump to conclusions, but I think those two are phonies."

"I suspected as much, Ursula, but what's their game? Are they really into quantum physics and multiverse travel? Let's check with Howard and Marlin. Meanwhile, any news on the Advanced Sustenance front?"

"Yes! Rachel is right. Advanced is playing above their competence. They have access to information, formulas and techniques they didn't develop in-house. I'm not sure they got it from *P&P* but the end products are very similar in design. I think we should pursue a leak here. We don't want to reveal me or my capabilities so why don't you follow up with Rachel. Who has access to the Burger and Wurst recipes? I suspect it's very few animals."

"OK, but in the meantime, let's alert Octavius and Belinda about the Turmoil situation and quiz Howard, Marlin and Bruce on what they know about the horses."

*****

Belinda shook her head. "I'm sorry I fell for their sociability ruse. Are they on a fact-finding mission? I should have gotten suspicious when Clarissa seemed very authoritative for a maid and wanted to share Multiverse information."

Octavius grunted. "I wish I knew what they are up to. Where are they now?"

They're having breakfast. Otto, Condo and the Twins are keeping them company. The Bold, Brave Bears are making a pitch for their film extravaganza and the Bird and Otter are being their entertaining selves. Little do they know Otto's history as a Multiverse traveler. *(See Book Seven – The Suit Case.)*

Condo was doing his vocal repertoire, imitating Clarissa's and Lucinda's voices. An Andean Condor as a thoroughbred - lots of laughs. Otto refrained from doing his "now you see him, now you don't" routine and stuck to wise-cracking his way through the conversation.

The Condor inquired, "Where did you study, Ladies?"

A short pause and Lucinda replied. "After I stopped racing, I got my doctorate in Quantum Physics at The University of Virginia - Clarissa only has a high school education." *(A patent lie as Ursula would soon confirm.)* And what about you, Senhor Condor?"

"I attended Universidade Estadual de Campinas (Unicamp) in Sao Paolo– I lectured on telecommunications there as well. Meu compadre, the Otter here, is a self-taught Canadian."

"Do either of you have any experience in Multiverse activities?" asked Clarissa, all too eagerly.

Otto, who could also lie convincingly, replied with paws crossed behind his back, "Afraid not, Ms. Mare. We're strictly earth creatures."

"So are we, unfortunately!" Clarissa's interest in the two of them was waning markedly.

"I would have thought General Turmoil would have let you in on his experiments. Aren't alternate universes one of his specialties."

Lucinda laughed, "Oh try getting Reginald to open up on the work he and his staff are doing. No such luck."

*****

"What do you know about them, Bruce?" This from Octavius.

"Not a zack, Ocko. I didn't get a chance to jabber much with them when I was at the Business and we couldn't talk much on the helicopter. General Turmoil introduced her as his wife and that ended it. Funny the way he referred to her. Almost as if he didn't know her. Odd!"

"Is she really his wife? Ursula can't find any evidence of a marriage."

"Can't prove it by me."

"Was there anything else strange about the General?

"Oh, come on, Ocko. He's one of the strangest blokes I've ever met."

"No! I'm serious. I would never have imagined in my wildest dreams that Turmoil would have gotten married. The fact that Ursula was stymied in her marital search makes me more suspicious. What about her maid who's not a maid."

"She's a Sneaky Sheila, all right."

Ursula chimed, "Something else, Doctor Bear. There is no Quantum Lady listed in any of the entries and results at US racetracks. I doubt she ever competed or even existed."

"Marlin and Howard! See what you can find out but don't give away anything vital. Take another Ursula with you. Who the Hell are they and what do they want?"

110

*****

(The Cubs had given up on their cinematic persuasion and Otto and Condo had departed the breakfast table conveniently leaving their Ursula behind on the sideboard running in passive mode.) When they thought they were alone, Clarissa turned to 'Mrs. Turmoil' and said. "We're going to have to be more careful. I think they may be getting suspicious."

"Well, we have to get active. We certainly didn't learn very much from that military fool. How much longer will his hypnosis last?"

"Only a few more days. This reconnaissance process is taking longer than we anticipated. Let's see what we can glean from the Porcupine and his waterlogged buddy. The Council won't be pleased if we can't tell them what they want to know. Those paranoid birds on Biosphere X *(See Book Seven -The Suit Case)* are convinced they are going to be obliterated by these Earthlings unless they strike first and totally. So far, the Council has been on a steady losing streak. We should never have taken on this contract. OK, here come our victims. Let's hope our spells work on them."

Howard entered the room pulling a portable wheeled tank containing Marlin. He also carried a laptop strapped around him in a routine fashion - Ursula.

Lucinda greeted them. "Good morning, Doctors. So kind of you to spare some time for us but we are absolutely fascinated by Multiverse travel. I have it on good authority that you two are the world's leading experts on alternate universes. I hate to admit it but Reginald and his staff don't seem to be in the lead. Would you agree?"

111

"I'm afraid we are not sufficiently knowledgeable of the Business' activities to comment on that, Mrs. Turmoil. They certainly devote a lot of time and resource on the subject but then so do we. I'm sorry we can't share our current and upcoming experiments with you but I'm sure you can see the need for confidentiality. We can discuss the materials we have published, of course."

Howard's Ursula had picked up the horses' conversation about hypnosis and Biosphere X from the one left behind by Otto and Condo and had warned him and Marlin. They decided to fake going into a trance and flushing out what the ladies had in mind. They both put on contact lenses to cut off any hypnotic influences. Swinging watches, anyone?

"I wonder, Doctors Watt and Dolphin, if you could identify this object for us. We are told it comes from an alternate world discovered by a member of the Business research team but we aren't sure. Perhaps you would recognize it. We've never seen one before."

She held up a metal cylinder resembling a flashlight with a lens on one end and shone it in the Octavians' eyes. A purple pulse glimmered. Marlin blinked several times and Howard shook his head. "Not familiar with it. What about you, Marlin?"

"Nope, but it does remind me of a device we ran into on *(nonexistent)* Biosphere K. Never could figure out what it was good for. How did you come by it?"

"It was a gift from an admirer. Oh, I'm so disappointed. I was hoping you could enlighten us. We think it's from Biosphere X."

"Aha," thought the Porcupine, "the light is beginning to dawn."

Staring blankly off into space, Marlin said, "We've had lots of dealings with Biosphere X all right. Nasty bunch! We thought they'd all been destroyed by the General. I guess <u>we'll</u> have to take care of it this time. Octavius is going to enjoy this. We've developed a new set of super weapons to deal with them. Those birds won't stand a chance."

Clarissa's jaw dropped. Finally! They can leave town, report back to the Council and collect their fee. Then they can say a permanent good-bye to Biosphere X.

"Oh, that sounds awful!"

"But necessary, ladies, necessary! Those cowards need another serious lesson. They never learn."

*****

The sudden disappearance of the horses from the Bear's Lair was not entirely unexpected. The "hypnosis" from the exotic flashlight had not affected Howard and Marlin courtesy of the contact lenses. They reported to Octavius that our guests had fled, believing they had uncovered a threat of impending catastrophe on Biosphere X if they attempted an assault on Earth Alpha. The birds would hesitate to unleash an attack if they were convinced they would be met by super weapon retribution. Uncharacteristically, the Great Bear informed the General, once he exited his state of hypnosis, about his "Wife's" deception. Turmoil was embarrassed and hardly pleased with being hoodwinked but was relieved to discover he was not married. He set off a search for Lucinda and Clarissa. No results. Needless to say, they could not be found at the Virginia mansion. The Cubs were disappointed they had lost two potential actresses for their film.

Chapter Nineteen

OK, Reader, it's time to insist
On providing this "tail" a last twist.
With an almost straight face
I'll wrap up the Wurst Case.
(I'm so sorry. I couldn't resist.)

Back to the *Pharm and Pharma* issues! While our brief interlude with the General's "wife" was progressing, the 'cultured meat' assessment was moving apace. The only jarring note thus far was a stray comment by one of the auditors about the close similarities between the experimental products of Advanced Sustenance and the offerings of Best Wurst and Best Burgers. He had been part of a pre-review of Advanced's planned patent submissions. They looked suspiciously similar to *P&P's* earlier submissions and his firm had refused to sign off. This is the first *P&P* had heard of the potential conflict. Octavius was obviously fiercely interested but nowhere near as excited as Rachel Raccoon and Paul Possum. Rachel was outraged. Paul was puzzled. They were convinced chicanery was afoot.

Ursula took it on herself to hack into the not yet public patent files of Advanced Sustenance even though that was borderline illegal. However, the likelihood of repercussions was unlikely, especially if the patents turned out to be stolen copies. They certainly looked like it. Both the product content and process engineering specs bore a remarkable similarity to *P&P's*. Some matched perfectly. That seemed pretty stupid. It was a dead giveaway.

"Paul and Rachel. Tell the auditors to recheck our product inventory. Advanced Sustenance probably has some of the product we created. They'll need it for patent submission.

"Victoria, put me through to the CEO of Advanced Sustenance. What's his name?"

"Wallace Wildcat. We've had trouble with him before. He and his staff are real jerks."

"Hello Mr. Wildcat? Will you please hold for Doctor Octavius Bear? Thank you!"

"Wildcat? Octavius Bear here. Sole owner and CEO of UUI and *Pharm and Pharma*. I think you should know that you and your company are in serious trouble. What? Theft of Intellectual Property; Probable Bribery; Suborning employees; Stealing equipment and product; Mail fraud; Patent violation; Misrepresentation of ownership – that's for openers. But we're just getting started. Criminal and civil violations. You're in our crosshairs and I have every intention of putting you out of business. See you in court and probably jail. Look me up. You'll find I'm a real hardass. I've already called the FTC, FBI, FDA, Patent and Trademark Office, Commerce and Agriculture Departments. *(A little exaggeration there but only in timing.)* No, I'm not interested in negotiating. Nine foot tall Kodiak Bears don't negotiate." He hung up.

"Well, that was fun but I'm really angry. Nobody screws with me."

Octavius summoned his two corporate lawyers and got them scurrying. Serena started preparing a list of possible damages and Wolford developed a series of 'cease and desist' orders.

"Now," said the Bear, "How did this happen? Somebody has been passing on secret and highly valuable information to a competitor. Who? How? Why? I can guess the Why. Those specifications alone are worth millions. Where's Jacques? Tell him I want to see him immediately. I want a list of everyone who has access to our specs, samples, plans and patents, inside and outside the company. Ursula, Maury, what have you got?"

"Whoever is doing this is pretty high up the tree. We're talking about information from a wide range of departments and processes that only a few people have access to. Either that or we have a conspiracy on our hands. I personally doubt it. Here comes Doctor Jackrabbit."

"What's up, Octavius? Did the audit uncover some kind of crisis?"

"Yes and No! There don't seem to be any problems with our processes or products and the financials and marketing seem OK. The Frau and Chita have come up with some outstanding diet and promotional approaches. No regulatory issues BUT Advanced Sustenance has copies of most of our confidential intellectual property. I'm going to sue the Hell out of them. Any light you can shed on that?"

Jacques pawsed.

"Come on, Jacques. Open up!"

"I don't want to speak ill of the dead but I think Llewellyn was padding his income."

"I hope you're not serious. I don't believe Llewellyn would do that."

"I'm sorry, Octavius, but I think that's why Llewellyn committed suicide. His death was no accidental overdose. His brother needed the money. His wife is very ill."

"So he sold out *P&P* to a competitor? And then had an attack of conscience? Are you sure of that?"

"Competitors! I had a session with him the night before he was heading for Washington. I told him of my suspicions and he admitted I was right. We agreed that he would go ahead and have his government conferences but then when he came back, he would resign. We'd come up with some reasonable excuse for his leaving. I didn't want him to be prosecuted. I don't know what he planned to do about Advanced Sustenance and the others. That had to be brought to the surface and stopped. I never thought he'd commit suicide but I guess he felt overwhelmed."

The Bear felt like he was hit by a thunderbolt. "OK, Jacques, thanks for being so open. I have to think this through. I'll be back to you."

When the Jackrabbit left, he said, "Ursula, Maury. Did you both hear that?"

"Yes," I said, "and I don't believe it. Let's check with Llewellyn's brother, Lewis. Is his wife really that ill? How sick was Llewellyn? Did they need money?"

"What do you think, Ursula?"

"Not sure! Maybe you ought to call Wildcat again and find out who his contact was."

"I may have burned that bridge. He's not going to say anything to me. Can you hack the records at Advanced again and see if there is any evidence of Llewellyn negotiating with them?"

"I'll try. They may have already destroyed the evidence."

I thought for a moment. "Has it occurred to you that Jacques may be covering for someone else?"

"Like whom, Maury?"

"Like him!"

"The thought did pass my mind. I don't think Llewellyn had readily available detailed access to all the materials that Advanced has. Rachel, Paul and Jacques are more likely candidates. Where is Victoria? I need to talk with her."

The PA came into the room. "Yes, Doctor Bear?"

"Victoria, I just got some disconcerting news, if true. Jacques Jackrabbit believes Llewellyn committed suicide. His death was no accident. Jacques thinks he was selling *P&P's* technology to a competitor or competitors. We know about Advanced Sustenance. There may be others."

"Oh! No way, Doctor Bear. Director Lama wouldn't do that."

"Do what?"

"Sell out the company or commit suicide. That's impossible. He loved *P&P* and he was scrupulously honest. I'd believe that of Jacques before I thought it of the Director. He was really jealous of Doctor Lama.

He felt Llewellyn was a useless figurehead and all the progress made by the company was under his direction. Rachel and Paul can't stand him. Llewellyn did suffer badly from diabetes, though. If he did commit suicide, it would have been due to his extreme neuropathy. But why now? What happened?"

"Good question!"

At that moment, Ursula rang her chime. "I've done some more research. As I suspected, Advanced Sustenance has disposed of their patent applications. I think you frightened Wallace Wildcat but Carver Institute is a likely candidate for Intellectual Property theft as well. No sign of any contact with Llewellyn but Jacques Jackrabbit was on their staff until three years ago. I uncovered some recent communications that mention joint development activities we don't know anything about. Check with Rachel and Paul. Then I think you may want to have another talk with the Hare."

"Good catch, Ursula. Thanks! Victoria, call in Rachel and Paul, will you."

It took a couple of minutes to round up the two specialists. Octavius spent the time reviewing the correspondence Ursula had uncovered between Carver's management and Jacques. Carefully guarded but certainly suggestive. Rachel came in first.

"To your knowledge, do we have any kind of mutual agreements with Carver Institute?"

The raccoon chittered. "Are you kidding? I wouldn't give them the time of day. Here's Paul. Ask him!"

"Ask me what?"

"Are we in bed with Carver Institute?"

"Not likely! Try Jacques. They're his alma mater. I don't like them. We're certainly not working with them. At least, I'm not. Are you, Rachel?"

118

A hiss from the Raccoon. "And one more time, we have nothing going with Advanced Sustenance, either."

"OK, you two can go. I'll talk again with Jacques." He whispered to Victoria. The he said, "Would you call Jacques back and then please go and do what I just asked you."

He called and asked the Colonel and Frau to join him.

The Assistant Director hopped back into Octavius' office. "What can I do for you, Octavius?"

"You could start by telling me the truth, Doctor Jackrabbit."

"Sorry?"

"Are you sorry? I have strong suspicions that it's you who's been shopping around our technology to other companies. Such as your former employer, Carver Institute."

"That's nonsense."

"You deny you have anything going with Advanced Sustenance and Carver Institute?"

"Absolutely."

"There's a letter of agreement in Carver's files that says otherwise and we have evidence of your misappropriating our property and giving it to Advanced."

"How did you get that?"

"Never mind! Still want to deny it?"

Another long pawse. "All right, I've been keeping them current on our progress but that's all. They are far behind us. I haven't turned anything over to them."

"I think otherwise. Would you care to restate your discussion with Llewellyn the night he left for Washington?"

"What do you mean?"

119

"Llewellyn accused you of selling out to competitors, not the other way around. He gave you a chance to resign and expected you to be gone by the time he returned from his government conferences. You weren't about to accept his ultimatum and told him so"

"That's nonsense."

"No, it's not. I have irrefutable evidence of your betrayals *(Ursula's hacks)* and I'm not going to hesitate to use them. I also believe you killed Llewellyn and I'm going to pursue that line of inquiry along with the Washington and Cincinnati Police."

Victoria came back and held up a bottle. The Bear nodded.

"We were wrong. Llewellyn didn't accidentally overdose. You murdered him. We'll start with the fact that you had and still have a supply of botulinum toxin in your possession. I asked Victoria to go just now and search your office and she found it hidden in your desk. Why you kept it, I don't know. For a scientist, Jacques, you're pretty clumsy and killing my friend is more than just clumsiness. It's vicious. I'm instructing the Colonel and Frau to hold you until the Police arrive. This wasn't what we intended when we organized this audit but it will do for at least one successful discovery. As far as Llewellyn's death is concerned, it confirms our wurst case scenario."

Epilogue

Hi, Maury here. Just to tidy up. The audit is complete and was effective. We've had our successful sessions with the government. The Frau and Roland Reynard have concocted some marvelous recipes. Chita and Ormand Oryx have a major marketing campaign planned out and in motion and *P&P's* products have hit the market with a bang. Lots of Obligate Carnivores are delighted. Jacques Jackrabbit is in custody accused of industrial espionage along with the officers of Advanced Sustenance and Carver Institute. He's also facing a murder charge. We still don't have a new Director of *P&P* but Octavius is getting tired. He's tried unsuccessfully to talk Belinda into the job. I'm not interested, either. Are you? Howard and Marlin still haven't located the two female horses and probably won't. The Cubs have a new project – an electronic game – Bold Brave Bear Ball. And this is really…

The End

About the Author

Harry DeMaio is a *nom de plume* of Harry B. DeMaio, successful author of several books on Information Security and Business Networks as well as the eleven-volume *Casebooks of Octavius Bear.* He is also a published author for Belanger Books and the MX Sherlock Holmes series edited by David Marcum. A retired business executive, former consultant, information security specialist, pilot, disk jockey and graduate school adjunct professor, he whiles away his time traveling and writing preposterous books, articles and stories.

He has appeared on many radio and TV shows and is an accomplished, frequent public speaker.

Former New York City natives, he and his extremely patient and helpful wife, Virginia, and their Bichon Frisé, Woof, live in Cincinnati (and several other parallel universes.) They have two sons, living in Scottsdale, Arizona and Cortlandt Manor, New York, both of whom are quite successful and quite normal, thus putting the lie to the theory that insanity is hereditary.

His e-mail is hdemaio@zoomtown.com

You can also find him on Facebook.

His website is www.octaviusbearslair.com

His books are available on Amazon, Barnes and Noble, directly from MX Publishing and at other fine bookstores.